BOOKS BY C.B. WILSON

Jack Russelled to Death

Cavaliered to Death

Bichoned to Death

Shepherded to Death

Doodled to Death

Corgied to Death (Coming 2023)

DOODLED TO DEATH

C.B. WILSON

DEDICATION

For Pamela Wright
the sister I chose

CONTENTS

1. Bow Wow Boutique
2. Posh Puppies
3. Bichon Bisquet
4. Beg-als Shoppe
5. Muttropolis
6. Woofing Best Coffe

7. Urban Pup
8. Snooty Pooch
9. Fluff & Buff
10. Fiesta Chihuahua

11. Bank
12. Gem's Palace
13. Blooming Tails
14. Taj Ma Hound

15. Hot Dog Stand
16. Bone Garden Salad
17. Attorney
18. Escrow
19. Hair Salon

Cat's Town House

Homes

K9 Fine Wine Bar

Graveyard & Ghost

Hounds Hardware

Frosty Pup

Chateau Chienn

Salty Dog Seafood

Doodle Pad

Mutt Hutt

Dogwo

KDOG Studio

Farmer's Market

A Lifeguard Tower

B

Dolce

Ciao Bella

Dog House

B Old Barkview Inn

WOOF

DOG PATH

2nd

3rd

4th

1st

DOG PATH

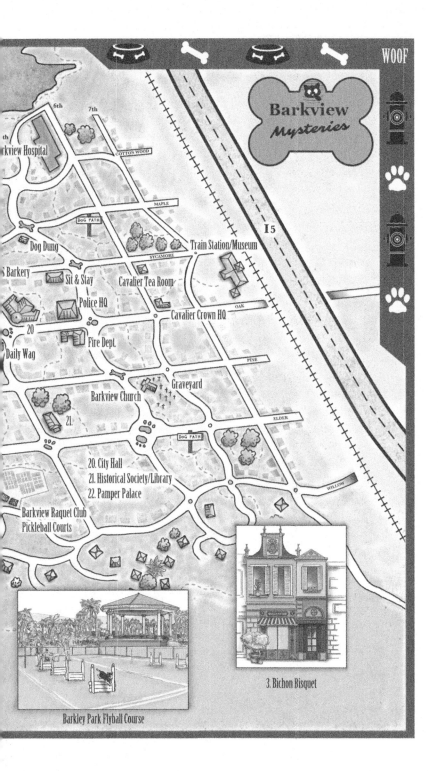

WOOF

Barkview
Mysteries

6th
7th
th
Barkview Hospital
COTTON WOOD
MAPLE
DOG PATH
Dog Dung
SYCAMORE
Train Station/Museum
Barkery
Sit & Stay
Cavalier Tea Room
Police HQ
I 5
Cavalier Crown HQ
OAK
20
Fire Dept.
Daily Wag
PINE
Graveyard
Barkview Church
ELDER
21.
DOG PATH

20. City Hall
21. Historical Society/Library
22. Pamper Palace

WILLOW

Barkview Raquet Club
Pickleball Courts

3. Bichon Bisquet

Barkley Park Flyball Course

CHARACTERS, HUMAN

Barklay, Celeste: Founder of Barkview in 1890.

Barklay, Charlotte (Aunt Char): Mayor of Barkview, dog psychiatrist on *Throw Him a Bone*. Renny, a champion Cavalier King Charles Spaniel, is her dog.

Barklay, JB: Aunt Char's late husband.

Barklay, Skye: 1920s aviator.

Douglas, Jonathan: Rumrunner lost in 1925. Owner of the Douglas Diamond. Married to Marie.

Duncan, Franklin: Old Barkview Inn concierge.

Felderhoff, Mitch: Owner of Muenster Milling. Grandpa Joe, a Golden Doodle, is his dog.

Gallardo, Peter: Biology teacher at Bark U. G-paw, a Golden Doodle, is his dog.

Garcia, Crack: World War I pilot and bootlegger.

Hawl, Russ: Cat's fiancé. FBI consultant. Owns Blue Diamond Security.

José: Manager of Barklay Kennels. Dog whisperer. Married to Ria.

Le Fleur, Michelle: Owns Fluff and Buff Salon. Fifi, a black Standard Poodle, is her dog.

Ohana, Lani: Cat's half-sister.

Ohana, Mary Ann: Cat's mother.

Oldeman, Edna: Skye Barklay's friend.

Oldeman, Will: Old Barkview Inn elevator operator.

Madame Orr: Barkview's fortune-teller/psychic. Danior, a Bedlington Terrier, is her dog.

Papas, Ariana: Owner of Gem's Palace Jewelry. Gem, a German Shepherd, is Ariana's dog.

Roma, Victor, Jr.: Chairman of Firebird Industries.

Schmidt, Gregory (Uncle G): Barkview's police chief. Max and Maxine, silver-point German Shepherds, are his dogs.

Smythe, Adam: Former mayor of Barkview.

Thomas, Dr.: Dean of the Science Department at Bark U.

Thompson, Jordan: Owner of the Sea Dog Dive Shop.

Turner, Gabby: Owner of the Daily Wag Coffee Bar. Sal, a Saluki, is her dog.

Williams, Chad: Treasure hunter searching for the Douglas Diamond.

Wright, Catalina "Cat": Producer/investigative reporter at KDOG. A cat person living in Barkview.

Wynne, Sandy: Cat's assistant and computer whiz. Jack, a Jack Russell Terrier, is her dog.

CHARACTERS, CANINE

🐾Danior: Madame Orr's Bedlington Terrier.

🐾Fifi: Michelle Le Fleur's black Standard Poodle.

🐾G-paw: (Grandpa Joe): Peter Gallardo's Golden Doodle.

🐾Gem: Ariana's German Shepherd.

🐾Jack: Sandy's Jack Russell Terrier.

🐾Max and Maxine: Uncle G's German Shepherds.

🐾Renny: Aunt Char's champion Cavalier King Charles Spaniel.

🐾Sal: Gabby's Saluki dog.

🐾Victoria (Tory) Rose (Queen Mum): The first Barklay Cavalier.

CHAPTER 1

Skye Barklay, Renowned Aviation Pioneer, a Murderer!

I crumpled the newspaper into a ball. Talk about inflaming the populace. I hate a sensational headline, especially when I hadn't written it. The investigation to induct this remarkable Barklay ancestor into the National Aviation Hall of Fame had certainly caused a dogfight in the dog-friendliest city in America.

Had Skye really murdered the missing rumrunner, Jonathan Douglas, and stolen the legendary Douglas Diamond to finance her adventures? The newspaper article had been vague on specifics, citing hearsay from an unnamed source. Where had this so-called evidence even come from? Was uncovering the truth even possible a hundred years later?

Part of me wished I hadn't started this witch hunt. I just had a driving need to expose hidden truths. My name is Catalina Wright, Cat to my friends. Clearly, I'd broken some Canine Commandment. Why else would someone want to deny this local heroine her due?

"This is..." Sandy Wynne, my millennial production assistant, filled my office doorway. She grasped her tablet like a Frisbee ready to toss.

Yup. She'd read the headline too. Like me, she'd dressed in herringbone slacks and a striped blouse. While she'd twisted her long blonde hair into a pencil-held bun, my tawny mane brushed my shoulders. Even Jack, her Jack Russell Terrier, growled at her feet. "...insane. Whose diary did the information come from?"

I wish I knew. I'd found Skye's travel trunk in my Aunt Char's attic, buried behind some retro 1970s furniture I'd been tasked to donate a few months ago. Of course, my reporter's mind had been drawn to the plethora of Depression-era travel labels. Mussolini's Italy, Peking the year Mao entered the Forbidden City gates, spy-infested Casablanca... The sheer adventure of it all spoke to me, but not as much as the feel of Skye's leather aviator's jacket hugging me close. Call it a quest. Her story had to be told.

"You need to fix this..." Sandy's forefinger reprimanded me with schoolmarm effectiveness.

"Me?!" I gestured around my office. No wood grain showed beneath the pile of programming and operational issues blanketing my desk. Being the general manager of KDOG, Barkview's only TV station, restricted my soapbox reach. My aunt Char, now Barkview's mayor, had made it look so easy. "The National Aviation Association's qualification investigators will see the evidence. If they find something, we will get a chance to refute it." As Aunt Char had reminded me just yesterday. "Interfering is grounds for permanent dismissal."

Sandy rolled her eyes. Rules had never stopped me before. "Someone doesn't want Skye honored."

No kidding. If I could figure out who, just maybe I could explain why. The whole conspiracy theory made no sense.

Skye's diaries spanning 1927–1946 read like a Hollywood block-buster. Backed up by flight logs, photos, and mementos lovingly packed in the trunk, each accomplishment had been verified by Jennifer Moore, Barkview's new librarian, allowing the National Aviation Hall of Fame selection committee to fast-track Skye Barklay's induction. I couldn't think of a soul who would want to taint this heroine's reputation. Unless it really was about petty jealousy aimed at the Barklays' legacy.

"It's unfortunate that our information on Skye only begins after the Douglas Diamond was lost. We have no idea how a disinherited heiress acquired an airplane," I said.

"There must be a reasonable answer," Sandy added.

I'm sure there was. I just didn't know it. Before I could frame an answer, the floor shifted beneath me. Just another aftershock. Not grounds to panic in Southern California.

Sandy scooped up Jack and joined me beneath the sturdy doorway arch. The shaking seemed equally as strong as last night's magnitude 5.5 quake that had dumped my reference books to the floor.

"See. Even Barkview's objecting." Sandy held Jack close, more to calm his nerves than her own.

Maybe the city was shaking its fist. Barkviewians stuck together. Our DNA demanded it. The Barklays and four other founding families had built this seaside Mayberry with their collective blood, sweat, and tears.

Listen to me, the last standing cat person in a town inhab-ited by over-the-top dog lovers, going on about community unity. It's not that I don't like dogs. In fact, over the past year, I've come to value a number of canine traits. However, I still prefer sleek, independent, and litter box–trained cats.

More likely, the quakes were the faults letting off a little steam. Not a bad idea for our little town either.

"Who builds a town on an earthquake fault anyway?" I

didn't expect an answer. Railing over one-hundred-and-thirty-year-old real estate choices solved nothing.

"I'd rather face a hurricane. At least then you get a warning." Maybe Sandy wasn't so calm after all. Her dainty little sneeze must've squeezed Jack since he whimpered in her arms.

"Aunt Char did warn us," I reminded her. Two days ago on her dog psychology show, *Throw Him a Bone*, to be exact. Who knew a natural disaster could manifest in a rash of dog anxiety, excessive barking, whining, and runaways? Maybe having all those pooches around had life-saving benefits.

Another shudder rattled our old Victorian office building, making the chandelier sway drunkenly. The room blurred around me, my reshelved books crashing to the wood floor in a synchronized thud. I grabbed the molding for balance.

"They're getting stronger." Sandy's matter-of-fact comment affected my pulse rate. "It's a foreshock. The worst is yet to come."

"A foreshock? Is that really a thing?" I tapped the US Geological Survey app on my phone. Of course it was.

"The most recent quake registered 5.6. According to this, it's within the margin of error. The next quake will tell us more," Sandy announced. "At least this building was built in 1907. It's survived its fair share of earthquakes."

"Including the 1925 quake that caused a bunch of the ocean caves to collapse. They had to have done something right." Barkview's long earthquake history even included a legendary missing diamond.

"I like the slow, rolling quakes better. It means you're farther away from the epicenter," Sandy announced.

"Really?" No reason to question her comment. Sandy tended to know everything. Besides, there was nothing rolling about these earth tremors—more like sharp jerking motions. Was that bad news? I didn't want to know.

Several minutes of teeth-clenching quiet ticked by. "Do you want to go home?" I asked. I might as well send the nonessential KDOG staff home. No one could focus in this mess. I'd finally found the first benefit of my new position.

"Okay. Let's..." My phone vibrated with a text alert. I glanced at the screen: a 911 message from my sister. Ugh! Could this day get any worse?

"What did Lani do now?" Sandy asked, suddenly all business.

I didn't question how she knew. I felt my jaw tighten as I dialed. Lani picked up on the first ring.

"Cat, I think he's dead." The line disconnected before I could even process her words.

Never quick to respond to an emergency, I just stood there dumbly staring at my phone until Sandy snatched it from my hand.

"Tracking her phone's location now." Sandy's calm penetrated my paralysis, and I raced back into my office to retrieve my car keys. I'd known allowing Lani to stay in Barkview after her unceremonious arrival three months ago had been a mistake. Chaos stuck to my half-sister like a bad hair day. A dead body? Could it be a biology class cadaver gone astray?

Sandy's comment crushed that hope. "She's at the Barkview Lagoon. Strike that. She's in the... Wait... The phone's dead."

Of course it was. "She's a lifeguard. She went in the water after the body."

"With her phone? That's..."

"Lani." Miss Act-Before-Thinking.

"She is young." Sandy's excuse failed to convince me. Twenty wasn't that young.

Sandy followed me out the door. "I'm coming with you. Someone has to stop you from strangling her."

No doubt a good idea. I must've been in another world not to object even when Sandy's dog, Jack, leaped into the front seat of my Jag SUV with us, triggering a blizzard of white needle-hairs that blanketed the black interior. I bit back a comment. The car wash could deal with it.

I turned right out of KDOG's driveway. First Street dead-ended at the Barkview Lagoon's south parking lot. "Can you tell where she was at the lagoon?"

Sandy typed on her phone. "You're not going to like this, but the last signal is on the northeast side."

"On private property?" Of course, she'd be trespassing too.

"Do they even have the signage up yet?" Sandy asked.

"That's not a legal defense." Sandy's head shake confirmed that my sister was definitely on restricted land. I yoga-breathed, praying for patience. "Call Uncle G."

"Uh... Are you sure you don't want to see what's going on first?" Sandy chewed her lower lip. No one called the chief of police without verifiable cause.

"No. I'm not sure. I do know if my sister thinks she found a dead body, she probably did."

Sandy started to speak but then stopped and placed the call. Uncle G's gruff voice emanated from the phone speaker. "Trouble runs in the family."

I tensed. Somehow he already knew about Lani. "This is your fault. I wanted to send her back to Mom in Hawaii. You and Aunt Char insisted she stay."

Uncle G's *harrumph* made me feel better. "Family."

More like half-family on my mother's side. Lani was no blood relation to either Uncle G or Aunt Char. Yet they'd both stepped up to support my wayward sister, no doubt for my benefit. Technically, Uncle G wasn't family either. As my aunt Char's second husband's brother-in-law, he qualified as a friend. Calling him "uncle" just made that explanation easier.

6

"Lani called you?" Why would she call 911 before me?

"She didn't. An anonymous caller tipped us off."

Foreboding stirred. I stepped on the gas, throwing Sandy and Jack back in the leather seats. "To what, exactly?"

"A dead body."

"A man or a woman caller?" I asked.

"Computer-generated voice."

Warning bells chimed in my head. I motioned Sandy to disconnect the call. No need to be reminded to stay away. I had no intention of obeying anyway. "I have a bad feeling about this."

No argument from Sandy, just a not-again sigh. I liked that about her. Good or bad, she always joined the adventure. "What do you need me to do now?"

"Look up the shortest route to Lani's last GPS coordinate."

Sandy had both of our phones programmed before I parked in the packed-sand-on-sandstone lot. Besides the Barklay Kennel Jeep Aunt Char had loaned Lani, a silver Prius was the only other vehicle in the lot.

I popped the trunk and pulled my court shoes out of my pickleball bag. Not the best for hiking, but better than the kitten heels I'd worn to the office. At least Sandy's sturdy boots helped her navigate the gravel trail.

She placed Jack on the ground and instructed him to track. A domesticated fox hunter? In a cloud of dust and a string of high-pitched *arfs*, the dog darted down the trail with Sandy right behind.

I followed at an adrenalin-induced walk-run, mostly ignoring my tender pickleball-injured knee on the pebbly path. Distant sirens kept the time constraints front and center.

Fortunately, following Jack's on-the-hunt bark proved simple. The trail led me east at Lagoon Fork past coastal sage groves mixed with California chaparral, then north through an unlatched and crookedly ajar shiny, steel gate. Proving Sandy's point, no signage marked the fence, but the new owners had staked their territory.

A louder, more aggressive bark drowned out Jack's as I sprinted past the scrub brush thicket. I found Sandy, biceps straining, holding back Jack's lunge toward a caramel-colored, dripping-wet dog three times his size crouched in attack mode and barking a Dirty Harry threat.

OMG! I recognized the Golden Doodle right away. Which meant my soaked sister was performing mouth-to-mouth on her biology professor!

CHAPTER 2

My head ready to explode for more reasons than the-can't-hear-myself-think barking, I took a lesson from my past three dog-sitting gigs and went alpha dog. "Quiet!"

It worked. Jack and G-paw, the Golden Doodle, quit mid-*arf*. Sandy stepped up and took charge of the canines. I think my sister even looked up. Hard to tell the way her dripping hair hid her face in classic Cousin Itt fashion. She did switch from rescue breathing to chest compressions on the guy wearing a black wetsuit.

I closed the distance between us, heedless of any possible evidence tampering. It took me a second to confirm the victim's identity. Without the distraction of horn-rimmed glasses and his ever-present dark-haired bedhead, Peter Gallardo looked quite fit for a nerdy academic on the backside of twenty who wore perpetually rumpled khakis and untucked shirts.

"Lani, he's gone." I didn't need to examine the body to know I was right. The sightless blue gaze and lips told the unnerving tale.

"N-no!" Her voice cracked. She doubled her chest compression pace.

If his heart hadn't already stopped, it would have exploded from the pounding. "Lani." I touched her shoulder. "You've done all you can."

"No. He can't drown. I'm a certified lifeguard. I save people..."

Her shoulders trembled as she sobbed. I pulled her into my embrace. My French-cuff blouse wasn't going to survive this encounter, I realized, as Lani's wetness seeped through. Although about my size and weight, she still seemed small in my arms. "What happened?" I brushed her stringy hair out of her face.

"G-paw knew something was wrong," Lani began. "As soon as I parked, he jumped across me to get out of the car and took off. When I got here, the dog was in the lagoon dragging Peter to the shore. I dove in and pulled him out the rest of the way. I don't know how long he'd been in the water. I..." Another sob ripped through her body.

I got it. No one should ever see a dead body. I'd freaked when I'd seen my first all those years ago in Los Angeles. The gruesomeness still registered, but not as traumatically. "Who was his scuba buddy?"

"He dove alone. I told him it wasn't safe." Lani swallowed. "He either swam or dove in the lagoon just about every day. I don't know why. There's nothing to see but boring rocks and an even-more-boring sandy bottom."

Said the girl whose father taught us both to dive in Hawaii. "You dove with him?"

"Sometimes. I mostly walked G-paw. Peter preferred to dive alone," she said, clearly miffed. "I really did remind him buddy diving was safer."

"Did you report this incident to the police?"

Lani shook her head. "No. I-I called you like you told me to do."

Then who had alerted them? My something-isn't-right alarm kicked up a notch. "Why did you come here?" I asked.

"I"—she hiccuped—"brought Peter his lunch." She pointed to a familiar Chateau Chien bag lying on its side in the swaying, hip-height Mexican beach grass.

Fancy French takeout on a college student's allowance? I needed to reevaluate her monthly stipend.

"He likes—liked—prosciutto and Brie on French bread," Lani explained.

Who didn't like crusty French bread and decadent Brie cheese?

"His grandfather imports wine from France, you know."

I did. She'd gushed about Peter Gallardo's dreamy blue eyes often enough since the semester started a few months ago. That bad feeling came back with a vengeance. "Did he call you?"

"N-not exactly."

A hedge on an easy yes-or-no question with a lip chew? I braced myself. I wasn't going to like this answer.

"G-paw ate Peter's lunch," Lani explained.

I glanced at the Golden Doodle practically stuck to Sandy's leg while Jack sat on her other side, glaring. "And you knew that how?"

"When Peter missed his scheduled office hours, I went to his bungalow and found his lunch bag on the kitchen floor."

"You have a key to his home?" Could this be more than a harmless crush?

"Yeah. I walk G-paw when Peter forgets."

Since Hollywood movies could have based their absent-minded professor characters on Peter, that had to be often. "So you decided to bring him lunch. How did you know he was here?"

"Well, I tried to call him."

"But?" My gut twinged a warning.

"When he didn't answer, I tracked him."

"Tracked him?" I repeated.

"Yeah. I activated the Find Me app on my phone." Her nonchalance bothered me the most.

"That's called stalking." Sandy's statement verbalized my thoughts exactly.

"I am not. Peter loses his phone three times a week." She rolled her eyes too innocently. "Tracking it is efficient."

"And illegal." Sure, I followed Lani for the same reason, but with her consent. "Unless he knew you were tracking him. Did he know?"

"We—uh—talked about it." The three-alarm fire on her cheeks answered that one.

Furballs! The police sirens sounded like they were minutes away, reminding me to speed up the interrogation. Clearly, more was going on with Lani and Peter than I'd thought.

"I'll call the lawyer," Sandy announced and dialed. That she had the number of KDOG's corporate lawyer on speed-dial implied something I didn't want to explore right now.

While I waited for Sandy's confirmation that legal counsel was on standby, my critical eye assessed the scene. The lagoon landscape included a narrow stretch of soft beige sand broken by the occasional boulder and clumps of twiggy chaparral. Inland, a line of eucalyptus trees offered a windbreak. A few feet from the mirror-like blue water, a scuba tank with a BCD and regulator octopus lay on the shore beside a balloon-tire wagon holding another unused scuba tank. A blue Igloo cooler separated two low chairs farther up the beach. Aluminum cans filled both cupholders. Mauve lipstick on one surprised me. Lani wore a pinker shade. Was something more going on here?

I lifted the cooler's lid. Crumpled sandwich wrappers and two banana peels lined the bottom. Peter hadn't been alone. Had Lani interrupted a cozy lunch?

"Was Peter dating anyone?" I asked.

Lani's blush said way too much. Ugh! How had I missed this one? "You're sure no one was here when you arrived?"

"Positive. G-paw would've barked at them."

That made sense. "Did you see another car in the parking lot?"

"No-o." Her jaw dropped as her eyes focused on the soda cans.

She hadn't known someone else had been here with Peter, I realized in relief.

Suddenly, Lani jerked out of my embrace. The cool offshore breeze sent a chill to my toes. Soaked from my neck to my waist, I had no choice but to wrap my arms around myself. Lani closed the distance to the chairs in three long strides.

"Don't touch it," I yelled. No need to tamper with evidence. Whoever had shared a drink with Peter had been the last person to see him alive. Uncle G needed to investigate.

Lani froze mid-reach. "That's not Peter's drink."

"How do you know?" Sandy quickly asked.

"Peter only drank out of cans with a spout." She must've seen my confusion because she continued, "He cut his tongue on a soda can as a kid and refused to drink anything from a can. His mom created the spout for him."

"Peter's mom owns Sipper Doodle Drinks?" Sandy asked.

Lani nodded. "She started the company for Peter. You'd be shocked how many kids get hurt on cans."

I cringed at the thought. If the drinks weren't Peter's, then whose were they? Something wasn't adding up. Time to take

13

notes. I patted my pockets, searching for my go-to Post-it notes. Nothing. As usual, Sandy came prepared. She handed me a pink pad and a pen. I thanked her with a nod. What would I do without her?

"Who would Peter come here with? You know this is private property now. He"—and whoever he'd been with, I added silently—"was trespassing."

"Peter had permission to be here," Lani insisted. "He was researching SSWS."

"What's that?" Ugh! Keeping up with acronyms drove me crazy.

"It's sea star wasting syndrome. A virus that killed a bunch of California sea stars," Lani replied.

"I thought Peter was a biologist," I said.

"He's actually an oceanographer with a biology degree. I told you he was smart."

My sister interested in a nerdy marine biologist? My mother was going to kill me.

"You know, I don't see Peter's Doodler anywhere," Lani said.

"A what?" Talk about confused.

"It's like an Etch A Sketch for adults. You know, a small computer." Her hands formed an eight-by-twelve rectangle. "Peter jotted all kinds of notes on it. He sketched on it too. It has to be here somewhere. He carried it with him everywhere." Sandy and I looked toward the water.

"In a waterproof case," Lani explained. "I added a bright red floating lanyard to keep it around his neck and make it easier to find."

She searched around the immediate area. In fact, we all looked, including G-paw, who nosed under the perimeter scrub brush. Not that he knew what we were looking for.

No Doodler. G-paw did find another soda can. This one had an unusual straw-like spout sticking out of it.

"Ha. Told you. That's Peter's Sipper Doodle." Lani reached for it.

"No. Don't touch it. It could be evidence."

She froze mid-grab. "More like Peter being a slob."

She should talk. Miss-Piles-of-Unfolded-Laundry-Everywhere.

Suddenly, Jack and G-paw crouched between us and the path and barked. Not a playful, happy sound, but a ferocious warning portending Uncle G's arrival.

Flanked by a pair of iron-gray search-and-rescue-trained German Shepherds that matched his neatly clipped beard and full head of hair, the police chief affirmed my theory that people chose physically similar canine companions. The silver epaulets on his navy shirt even coordinated with the dog's official police vests.

Uncle G's situation analysis took less than a minute. In a single hand wave, he motioned his deputy dogs to guard the perimeter, the EMT to take charge of Peter, and Lani, Sandy, and me to stand aside. We gathered around the nearest low boulder and sat down to wait. Sandy held a squirming Jack, while G-paw leaned against Lani's thigh. Not the most comfortable perch, but she endured until All-American officer Richie Richards supplied us with blankets. Six feet and a bunch more in height, Richie's linebacker build intimidated on sight. Fortunately, his boyish smile made him easy to get along with.

I snuggled into the warm fleece. It felt like heaven. Non-Barkviewians didn't understand that the offshore breeze on a cloudy day in May cut through you like an arctic freeze. Well, maybe not that bad, but more than capable of raising goose bumps. Of course, Lani wrapped G-paw in her blanket, holding the dog security-blanket tight. Uncomfortable as it looked, G-paw stood there sharing his warmth. I shivered, less from actual cold than concern for my little sister. Something was seriously off here.

My unease escalated as I watched Uncle G examine the scene and hone in on the lipstick-stained can. Real fear stirred in my stomach as he marched toward us, his toothpick twirling like a top between his lips. Just wait until he found out Lani had been stalking the victim.

I tried to point him toward the Sipper Doodle can. "G-paw found it. We didn't touch it."

Uncle G motioned Officer Richards to bag the can as evidence, never breaking eye contact with my sister. So much for diverting him. "What happened, Lani?"

Unaccustomed to Uncle G's military investigative persona, my sister's deer-in-the-headlights gape had disaster written all over it.

Suddenly, my innate reporter's curiosity vanished, replaced by a mama-bear protectiveness. I stepped between Uncle G and Lani as if I could protect her. "No questions until the lawyer arrives. He will confirm everything is legal."

Uncle G just about roared.

"But I didn't do anything," Lani's voice squeaked.

"Then you have nothing to be worried about." Uncle G's growl cut off my next comment.

Not to be deterred, I glared back. "No questions without counsel present. It's the law."

Uncle G's cough did not fully disguise his cuss. He faced Lani. "Are you invoking your right to an attorney?"

I nodded at my sister's questioning look. "I, uh, guess." If she waffled here, I'd kill her myself. If my mother didn't beat me to it.

"Yes or no?" With his arms crossed, Uncle G looked unmovable. His are-you-sure glance fueled my doubts. Was I too emotionally involved in this to think clearly? Uncle G would settle for nothing but the truth. He'd get it too. Just not at Lani's expense.

"Y-yes," Lani said.

The chief motioned Officer Richards to cuff her. Seriously? As if Lani was a flight risk. The intimidation worked. Lani looked ready to faint.

Peeling G-paw out of her arms about caused a dog fight. Between G-paw's don't-even-think-it growling and Uncle G's alpha-dog attitude, the standoff intrigued me. Eventually, G-paw backed down and obeyed with an under-protest yap.

"No one touches anything here." Uncle G's sweeping gesture included both Sandy and me. "You two get out of here. No witness collaboration."

Sandy bit her lip. She didn't want to leave Lani either. "What do we do?" she whispered for my ears only.

"Figure out who was on the beach with Peter," I replied. My way-too-trusting little sister had stepped in a pile this time. The way it looked, I'd be a witness for the prosecution. When my mother found out... I couldn't breathe. She'd made it clear I couldn't be trusted to protect Lani. Had she been right?

No. I could fix this. I just needed to focus. "She needs dry clothing," I announced. An orange jumper wasn't an option.

"Bring what she needs to the police station in one hour," Uncle G barked. "And take that Golden Doodle."

Peter's dog? I really was destined to house jailbirds' dogs. G-paw barked at my frown. No way he knew what had just happened. Or did he? In his paws, I wouldn't want to go with me either. At least Lani seemed relieved. Not about her own safety, but about G-paw and his care.

I hugged Lani close and whispered, "It will be okay. I'll find whoever was at the beach with Peter."

"I know..." Her confidence helped. "Find Peter's Doodler. It was his lifeline." She slipped a key into my hand. Had to be to Peter's house. I already had keys to her dorm. At least she grasped her peril.

Suddenly, I knew I'd find that Doodler. But the real answers wouldn't be that easy. The real question was, who was Peter Gallardo and why had he been in Barkview?

CHAPTER 3

KDOG's corporate attorney arrived just as Lani ducked her head into Officer Richards' patrol car. I felt better knowing the lawyer would watch out for her while I hunted down answers. Sandy drove Lani's car to the KDOG studio and left it there; Jack was under guard in her office.

Together we headed east to Bark U in my vehicle. Although G-paw sat in the back seat, the top of his head blocked my view of Sandy, bringing a whole new meaning to riding shotgun.

On campus, Sandy directed me down a meandering side road around Ivy League–style brick buildings to the professors' quarters that were located in a block of quaint Craftsman bungalows remodeled to be duplexes tucked into the hillside bluffs. No ocean views from this location, just swaying eucalyptus and scrub brush framing a grassy park with strategically-placed rock benches. And no problem finding Peter's residence, thanks to G-paw. The dog leaped out of my Jag, nearly knocking me over, and galloped up the path leading to the right. Sandy and I had to run to keep up.

Sandy had no problem, but I huffed all the way to the last single-story tan building. I paused on the shaded porch beside the comfy swing. Before I could fish out the key, G-paw nosed his way right through the doggie door. Sandy followed. I did, too, questioning if I'd make it through when my hips jammed half in, half out. Just the thought of explaining this to Uncle G gave me the last push to make it. Thankfully, I'd skipped the bloat-inducing pasta lunch I'd planned.

The tornado-trail chaos inside stopped us at the entry. Sofa overturned and bookcases emptied onto the floor meant someone had done a thorough job. I shared a glance with Sandy.

"The Doodler," we said in unison. "Don't touch..."

I turned to leave. No way I'd chance a tampering-with-evidence charge to look for the elusive Doodler in that mess. Better for Uncle G's forensics team to search.

G-paw had another plan. He took a direct route to the refrigerator. No way I'd have believed it if I hadn't seen it myself. With a quick twist of his front paw and a pull with his nose, he swung one of the side-by-side stainless steel doors open. I gasped as he stood on his hind legs and nosed around each shelf before he drew back a cheese wedge—cheddar, based on the color. Sharpness unknown.

Sandy whistled. "Impressive."

No kidding. That dog had talent, all right. Good or bad? Depended on what the dog ate, I guess. I made a mental note to store all my favorite foods on the top shelf out of his reach.

"He'd have to be pretty self-sufficient around Peter," Sandy remarked.

No argument from me. Peter having a dog made no sense. According to Lani, the guy barely took care of himself.

"G-paw, come," I said.

His you're-kidding-me brown-eyed glance taunted me.

Sandy pointed to her feet. "Come, boy. Let's go."

I swear the dog sighed and then gobbled the cheese snack in a single bite. Tail wagging, he jogged to Sandy's side. No question, G-paw had been trained. He just didn't obey well.

Sandy gestured to the doggie door. G-paw slipped right through and took off again across the grass. She bolted after him, while I followed as quickly as my injured knee allowed. The dog wove in and out of the ivy-covered buildings until he arrived at the Science Hall. Built from locally crafted sandstone, the building occupied a premium ocean view lot to the west.

Sandy sat on a stone bench beneath a colorful stained-glass window depicting a microscope, with G-paw at her side. No problem locating Peter's office, either; the dog led us right to it, across the hall from YouTube treasure hunter Chad Williams' closet-with-a-view office. The key Lani had given me opened Peter's office. Although the room had no windows, it did have a couch and conference table lit by a skylight offering an abundance of sunshine.

G-paw maneuvered around the desk and leaped into Peter's chair. With his front paws on the desktop, he looked more like a shaggy-haired executive than a pet. I swallowed my laugh as Sandy went right for the desktop computer. She cracked her knuckles like the pro she was and leaned over G-paw to type. If anyone could figure out Peter's password, Sandy could. I thumbed through a pile of dusty leather-bound books. Curiously, all were on loan from the Barkview Library's historical collection and referenced the years 1920–1930.

Why was a visiting marine biologist reading about the Roaring Twenties? Sandy's "Aha!" coincided with the top of the hour's last bong of the clock tower. She'd cracked Peter's password. Too bad we were out of time, if we had any hope of meeting the chief's timetable. "Buy me ten minutes." She whipped a thumb drive off her keychain.

I swallowed my objection. She'd done the hard part. I quickly texted and then dialed my aunt, praying she'd answer. Not that she routinely ignored my 911 calls, but as the sitting Barkview mayor, her response wasn't always timely. It was today.

"Lani has been arrested?" Aunt Char asked.

It wasn't really a question. She knew. If the info was interesting enough, Barkview gossip traveled faster than a 5G-enhanced alert. "She's only being questioned about Peter's death. No time for an explanation now. I need you to occupy the chief for the next twenty minutes."

"I understand." Somehow she'd make it happen too. "I just spoke with Ariana. I imagine she will be sending you a Golden Doodle charm for your bracelet." On that note, my aunt disconnected the call.

Our local jeweler had gifted me with a charm bracelet to commemorate my now-numerous dog-sitting experiences. She'd called it my journey bracelet. I frowned at G-paw's fluffy head propping up Sandy's chin. I supposed he was the next dog in my quest to discover if a canine mate existed for me. It really had to be some cosmic joke. Dog-sitting for three breeds already wasn't enough?

I considered the fluffy dog filling the computer chair. What wasn't to like about a self-sufficient, hypoallergenic cuddle monster? Could this dog be my perfect companion?

My diamond engagement ring twinkled in the sunlight, reminding me that my opinion wasn't the only one that mattered. I wasn't alone any longer. Although he worked in Los Angeles, Russ Hawl would drop everything if I called for his help. He'd recently become a partner in a government-contracted security company, and the secretive nature of his work still made me crazy.

Sure, my current management position might be considered boring, but deep down I was an intuitive investigative reporter. And my instincts were telling me not to underestimate Peter Gallardo. I flipped through the library books, photographing the bookmarked passages. No common theme jumped out at me. Hopefully, our librarian, Jennifer Moore, could offer some insight.

Finally, Sandy shooed G-paw to the ground. "Let's go."

I breathed easier as we power-walked to my car. In the car, Sandy popped the jump drive into her laptop. "Yeet! Peter's a treasure hunter after the Douglas Diamond."

No real surprise there; half of Barkview's visitors were these days. But why hide behind a nerdy academic exterior? After a wannabe king offered a million-dollar finder's fee for recovering the Douglas Diamond, fortune seekers flocked to Barkview determined to find that hundred-year-old treasure. Add a prophecy portending success within a narrow window of opportunity, and overnight our charming seaside village changed into a mecca for reckless behavior and trespassing. No wonder the chief viewed visitors with suspicion. But accuse my sister of murder? Not going to happen.

I refused to read too much into the weird maternal instinct driving me. I'd help anyone wrongly accused. Sure, the wrath of Mary Ann factored in. Despite my mother's low opinion of my babysitting skills, Lani's situation couldn't be entirely dumped at my door. Finger pointing aside, finding answers seemed like the most productive solution.

"What else did you find?" I asked.

"The usual 1911 topographical map. World War II blasting maps. A new construction map of Barkview Village circa 1922.

Did you know the beach in front of the Old Barkview Inn was called the Rising Sun Beach back then?"

I shook my head. An East Coast beach, sure, but Barkview's beaches faced the sunset. "Any idea why he was diving in the lagoon? There's nothing to see there."

"Not a clue. It gets even more odd. He has a file on 1930s dam projects in Southern California and a random drawing of a house on a jetty that can't be from Barkview."

"What kind of house?" I squealed my brakes at Elm Street's corner, speeding toward police HQ.

"A three-story brick house in the late mansard style with a cool red door," Sandy replied.

"A red door?"

"Yeah. A bright red door," Sandy emphasized. "No idea where it's located, though."

"You're sure it couldn't be an old Barkview home?"

"Not this one." Of course she was sure. I should believe her too. "It's brick with a north-south ocean view."

"A home in the Terraces?" Most of Barkview's ocean-view lots were located on the hillside above the famous Barkview ocean caves where Jonathan Douglas supposedly stashed his booty.

My suggestion initiated another head shake. "It's definitely on a jetty like a lighthouse would be. Would also be a great lookout." To prove her point, Sandy adjusted the screen angle for me to see too. No such luck. I saw a sliver of red over G-paw's curly beige head. I stretched my neck. That bright red door caught my eye. I swerved right. Sandy and G-paw collided.

My sharp correction wasn't fast enough. The front tire jumped the roundabout curb, plowing toward the freshly planted zinnias. I jerked the wheel. Sandy's gasp barely registered as I quickly straightened the wheels onto the pavement and darted into the visitors' parking lot at police headquarters. Thanks to my lead foot, we'd made it to police headquarters with a minute to spare. I parked beside the KDOG lawyer's car. Phew, I'd missed the flowers. Had to love my high-performance SUV.

Too bad my passengers didn't share my enthusiasm. Sandy ended up seat-belted to the door with G-paw sprawled across her lap, his big paws wrapped around her neck, drool dripping down her shirtfront. Ick!

I jumped out of the vehicle and ran to the passenger side to pry the dog off Sandy's lap. Sandy's pale-faced skyward prayer coupled with G-paw's shaky legs really aggravated me. Oh, come on. It hadn't even been a close call.

I shook off their concern and detoured to my pickleball bag. Lani would have to wear my I Heart Pickleball shirt and creased workout joggers. At least they were clean. Explaining our detour to Peter's residence promised to be more painful than a questionable fashion choice. We had a clue too. No Barkview home fit the picture of the house Sandy had uncovered. I couldn't even determine the exact location. As far as I knew, no land mass offering a north-south water view jutted out into the ocean anywhere near Barkview. So where was it? And why was Peter interested in it?

It really would be the perfect lookout. I even imagined a signal light shining on foggy nights in one of those third-floor windows. In the 1920s the upper floors would've likely been servant's quarters, the folks least interested in Prohibition and easily bribed by an affable Jonathan Douglas. Time for a deep dive into Barkview circa 1920.

CHAPTER 4

Officer Richards took the clothing for Lani and statements from me and Sandy. That the chief had Lani in an interrogation room didn't surprise me. Not excusing himself to berate me personally did. Something more was going on here. I sensed it.

Free to go, Sandy chose to walk the four blocks to KDOG to clear her head before producing tonight's show. Her I-need-air excuse made perfect sense after another tremor shook pens and nerves at the police station. Although it was less intense than the last, I still prayed the aftershock phase would go quickly. A major earthquake would not be a good thing.

G-paw and I could've walked across the grassy dog park to the Barkview Library, but further avoiding Uncle G made more sense. I chose to move my car. Convincing G-paw to ride along took more cajoling than anticipated, including half a power bar as a bribe. This sharing-food thing wasn't working out so well for me.

G-paw finally crouched low in the front seat, his front paws anchored beneath him, his wary eye on me. I bit back a laugh as I put the car in drive and basically rolled the vehicle the block and a half to the tan-shingled Victorian originally built with proceeds from Jonathan Douglas's bootlegging bounty.

The three-story mansion occupied a full city block that in its time had enjoyed unobstructed Pacific Ocean views. Today, Barkview had grown around it. Only the upper-story widow's walk connecting dual spirals still looked out over the water and Barkview caves—the same caves Jonathan supposedly took refuge in with his treasure. His youngest daughter had donated the property to the city when a 1960s wildfire destroyed the original library.

Some might call the sacrifices made in the name of finding this treasure spanning over a hundred years a curse—from Jonathan's wife, Marie, who reportedly paced on that widow's walk every day until her death in 1940-something, praying for his return, to his great-granddaughter, Jan, who'd been murdered after she'd stumbled on another deadly secret in search of the diamond. The time had come to find that treasure and end this quest once and for all.

Another quake trembled beneath our feet as G-paw and I walked up the pansy-bordered path to the library's front door. Jennifer Moore met us in the entry, her twin ruby Cavalier King Charles Spaniels flanking her. Today Jennifer had forgone her signature matronly bun and let her bouncy dark hair brush her shoulders. Her Spaniel-brown eyes danced with an inner mischief that seemed contrary to her conservative fortyish spinster persona. The dark slacks and flowing floral print blouse she wore felt light and fun.

G-paw's reaction stunned me. He sat at my side with his head cocked to the right and stuck his tongue out at the prissy cavaliers who, in turn, tossed their heads and gave him their haughtiest shrugs. I swear G-paw's *arf* sounded like a chuckle.

"Welcome, Cat. How is your sister? The chief can be quite intimidating when provoked," Jennifer said.

27

I had to wonder when Jennifer had experienced that side of Uncle G's personality, which he generally reserved for repeat offenders, namely me. The current president of the Cavalier Crown Committee, which administered Barkview's annual Cavalier King Charles dog show, and the most efficient organizer I had ever encountered, Jennifer had shocked the whole town when she'd accepted the librarian's position. In the past few months, she'd turned our small-town library into a destination center for historical research.

The gossip superhighway was functioning at Autobahn speed today. "I don't know. I'm not allowed to see her."

Jennifer patted my hand. "I can't believe Peter is dead. How...?" Her eyes misted. Something more than casual interest on her part?

"We won't know until the autopsy report, but it looked like he drowned."

"Drowned?" Jennifer ushered me across the parquet floor and into the parlor-turned-book-lined reading-room. Except for a fancy multifunctional coffee machine, Victorian elegance surrounded me in true Eastlake style. The green-striped sofas coordinated with printed wallpaper and cushy Oriental rugs.

Jennifer headed for the coffee maker. "The Ladies Auxiliary Book Club finished the last of the caramel flavoring, but I can offer you a café mocha with cinnamon."

I nodded. "Soymilk will be fine, with a dash of nutmeg." Now I remembered her coffee addiction. She'd named her precious dogs after the two spices.

The rich odor of the Woofing Best Coffee brewing wrapped its warmth around me, and I shivered, remembering Lani's damp hug earlier. "Why does Peter's drowning surprise you?"

Jennifer took a deep breath. "The man swam relay for Texas A&M undergrad."

"Really?" Not very geeky of him.

"Why would I make that up?"

She wouldn't. "Anything can happen underwater. That's why you dive with a buddy."

"The water isn't deep in the lagoon. And I hear he was wearing a buoyant neoprene wetsuit."

She had me there. If in trouble, he could've just dropped his weights and floated to the surface.

"The girls"—Jennifer gestured to the Cavaliers hugging her ankles like fluffy slippers—"and I enjoy sunrise beach walks. I saw Peter and G-paw most mornings at the lagoon. G-paw usually bounded in and out of the water chasing him. That dog is such a clown. When Peter dove, G-paw would paddle above him and duck under." Jennifer's smile showed pure enjoyment. Not the first time the Golden Doodle had had that effect on people.

"G-paw swims too?" Lani had said that G-paw was trying to pull Peter out when she arrived.

"He is part Golden Retriever, you know."

And part Poodle. Hence the name Golden Doodle. "Why the lagoon?"

"I asked Peter the same question. He said he was studying the starfish wasting disease. Which explained why he wore a full scuba mask even when swimming."

It certainly provided a reason to search the lagoon's bottom. Although the tidal change refreshed the saltwater, river runoff still made the water brackish, marring the visibility. "Was he there every day?"

"I didn't see him every day. Doesn't mean he wasn't there. He swam in different places. One day he'd be on the south side. The next day farther up the beach, and so on. I once teased him that he swam around the entire lagoon," Jennifer chuckled.

Not so far off. "What did he say?"

29

"He blushed and said he liked to be thorough. He swam in a pattern of sorts. I don't know if he found anything."

Neither did we. We needed his Doodler. Still, why swim in the lagoon? The Barkview Cliffs were miles to the south.

"Did you see Peter today?" I asked.

"Yes. It was 8 a.m. precisely. I remember because Peter had just arrived with two chairs and I didn't see Lani or G-paw."

Peter had been at the lagoon for hours before Lani showed up. "Was anyone else with him?"

"Not that I saw. He invited me to sit while he suited up." Jennifer blushed.

Was she the unknown visitor? Her mauve-colored lipstick could be a match to the lipstick on the can. "Did Peter offer you one of his sodas?"

"He did, but I am not a Sipper Doodle kind of person. I don't care if his mother started the company. I brought my own." She pointed to a metal thermos.

I understood that. Caffeinistas had standards. I exhaled, glad Jennifer hadn't been his rendezvous. "I'm hoping you can tell me what books he came in here for." I gestured around the room.

"I really shouldn't. Librarians have a strict policy, but since you're looking for a murderer..." Jennifer smiled. "He read everything we had on Barkview in the 1920s. He was specifically interested in resident diaries."

"That seems weird for a biologist," I said.

"I thought so too. Especially when he said he was looking for references to flowers. When he finally confessed that there may be a link between the flowers and the wasting disease, it all made sense. Back in the Victorian era, flowers were a language of their own. Many a man conveyed his true feelings by sending the perfect posy."

"A custom ended by the social revolution of the Roaring Twenties," I added.

"Alas, you are correct. The Great War changed many things, including good manners. Women did continue to press flowers, though."

An excuse for a guy to want to read the teenage musings of a bygone era? "Any lady in particular interest him?"

"Skye Barklay."

I set my coffee on the coffee table cozy. "Was Peter her challenger?" OMG! Could he have been murdered for trying to disqualify Skye's Hall of Fame entry?

Jennifer's steaming coffee thudded on the table. This promised to be good.

"I don't think so. He wanted information from before 1925. Peter believed prolific writers like Skye don't just start journaling one day."

"We agreed with him," I said.

Jennifer stroked each Cavalier in turn. "Your point that Skye may have had nothing to write about while living in Barkview made sense."

"She had left Barkview by 1925 and was the youngest female pilot at twenty years old. By 1927 she was flying tourists to the Grand Canyon."

Jennifer exhaled. "I agree. Besting Amelia Earhart in 1929 in the first women's National Air Derby from Santa Monica to Cleveland was noteworthy too. So was flying solo across the Atlantic in 1934."

"Do you really think Sky Harbor Airport in Phoenix was named after her for her daring Grand Canyon rescue in 1927?" We hadn't been able to prove that little tidbit, yet.

"I know in here." Jennifer pressed her fist into her heart. "It is true. Any woman brave enough to test-pilot those experimental airplanes had guts."

Or a death wish. I never could piece together why I thought that. Women weren't allowed to fly missions back then, but there were indications she had—the most dangerous ones. "Did Peter find anything new?"

"He also focused on Marie Douglas and Sally Tomlinson."

"Every treasure hunter looks into Marie," I said, unimpressed. Marie's diary held some clue to the Douglas Diamond's hiding place. Don't ask me how I knew. I just did. "Who was Sally Tomlinson?"

Jennifer's deep breath had lecture written all over it. I leaned in, ready for insight.

"The woman Peter thought had betrayed Jonathan."

Now this was big news. "What about the Mexican pilot run out of town and deported?"

"Peter told me that the pilot was a scapegoat. Sally was the go-no-go relay."

"A what?"

"Her home was a perfect lookout. Her husband built the house to watch for the tuna fleet's return to port so he would know whether to staff his cannery."

"That's a brilliant idea," I remarked. If only staffing KDOG could be as easy. "Was the house brick with a red door?"

"Yes. The house was destroyed in the 1925 earthquake. Except for a few fuzzy, black-and-white coastline photographs, no pictures exist of the home that I know of today."

With the exception of the picture in Peter's files. How had he known about it? "What signal told the workers to go to the plant?"

"One light in the upper window. Two meant no fish for the day."

An easy code to remember for Jonathan's nefarious activities. "Could Sally have betrayed Jonathan?"

"Not likely. Sally was Jonathan's aunt and a Tomlinson by marriage. Her late husband started the cannery."

Family loyalty on both sides. No wonder she had been trusted by both Jonathan and the Tomlinson rumrunners.

"Sally left Barkview with all the Tomlinsons less than a month after Jonathan's disappearance. Of course, her house was destroyed in the earthquake."

"Where exactly was the house?"

"I would guess what remained of it after the earthquake is underwater near the lagoon's ocean entrance."

I blinked. That made no sense. "How is that possible? The quake wasn't that strong."

"The earthquake destroyed the house. It was shaken off its foundation. Probably just stayed there until Roosevelt's New Deal funded a dam project originating in the east county."

A light went on. "Like the Tennessee Valley Authority?" I still remembered bits of high school history.

"Exactly. Tourism drove a big chunk of Southern California's revenue. The Depression hit the area hard. The dam channeled water from inland streams and flooded the pre-1930s lagoon beaches. I think the water level rose about twenty feet."

"You mean there are buildings underwater in the lagoon?" No wonder Peter was swimming in there.

"Theoretically. It's been ninety years of saltwater degradation."

"Were there cliffs off the lagoon?" Could we all have been looking in the wrong place for Jonathan's caves all along?"

"I suppose it's possible. The coastline is full of cliffs and caves."

"Why didn't the 1911 map show the changes in topography?"

"It does. I hadn't seen it either. The lagoon shape didn't

change much. The size did when the water levels rose about twenty feet."

A twenty-foot difference? I should've seen that. "I still should've noticed the spit of land with Sally's house on it."

"It's the lagoon entrance now. The house was built in 1915 and destroyed in 1925. Why Sally's husband insisted on brick in earthquake country, I have no idea."

So many things weren't adding up.

"Skye also left Barkview about the same time." Jennifer's bombshell suddenly made all the accusations against Skye possible.

Coincidence? Not a chance. Skye had played a part in Jonathan's disappearance. I just knew it.

"It broke her mother's heart. Celeste had already lost her eldest son at Ypres during the Great War in a plane crash. To lose her daughter to the lure of air travel, I can't imagine," Jennifer said.

Or something else. *What* intrigued me exactly as Jennifer intended. I wouldn't stop until I discovered the truth.

"Skye did some amazing things, and she should be honored. I'm almost sorry I started this deep look into her past." The last thing I wanted to do was taint Skye's legacy.

"Never say that!" Jennifer's shock helped steady me. "History is a wonderful thing. Extraordinary people do ultimately get their just rewards. Sometimes it just takes the right person to discover the real story."

Assuming I was that person. Skye Barklay had challenged the system and won. My reporter's mind loved this kind of story. I'd also never allowed a criminal a pass. Jennifer knew that.

The real question was, how did Peter Gallardo know so much about Skye Barklay and the events leading up to Jonathan Douglas's disappearance on June 29, 1925?

Ready to leave, I expected G-paw to be a rug at my feet. Instead, the leash just dangled from my hands. No dog attached. What? I hadn't unclipped it.

This had to be a joke. I shot Jennifer a sharp look.

"Don't look at me like that. Poodles are smart dogs. G-paw's half Poodle."

Too smart for me is what she meant. Was G-paw some sort of escape artist? I refused to be beat. He had to be here somewhere. Years of producing my aunt's dog psychology show had taught me that dogs viewed life as a game. Was G-paw just playing hide-and-seek?

I peeked under the table, in the corner, in the hallway. No G-paw. When had he snuck away?

"G-paw, come." Despite my efforts, concern still creeped into my voice. Lani would kill me if I lost that dog.

The Cavaliers' ears perked. Not even a growl from G-paw. I yelled the command. He had to be here somewhere. He couldn't just leave the library, unless... "Do you have a doggie door?"

"Of course. This is Barkview," Jennifer replied.

Ugh! Real fear set in. He could be anywhere. Where did I even start to look for him?

Jennifer stilled my building panic. "I have an idea." She smiled and motioned for me to follow her up the ornately carved center staircase.

I barely noticed the banister as I trailed behind, focused instead on Jennifer's Cavaliers, who perfectly matched her pace. Who knew whether I'd one day crave that kind of attachment?

On the second level, Jennifer bypassed two doors before entering what must have once been a girl's bedroom, judging from the floral wallpaper. Instead of a frilly canopied bed and mirrored dresser, four dark wood bookshelves lined the room.

Jennifer headed right for the window. G-paw lay on the floor, acting like a footrest in front of a wing-back chair. His head cocked as if to say, "What?" My breath escaped in a rush. He hadn't run away.

"Poor baby. He misses Peter." Jennifer scratched his head. G-paw plopped his head back down on the wood floor, his collar clicking as it touched.

"This is the diary and memoir section. Peter spent many hours in this room," Jennifer explained.

So, in addition to everything else, I had a depressed dog on my hands. Great. Next stop: Aunt Char's. She'd know how to calm G-paw. At least I'd found him.

I leashed the Golden Doodle. The shelved books drew my eye as I prepared to leave. Some were leather, while others had been bound in cheerful floral prints. None matched in size or page quantity either. The aged pages looked faded and hard to read. "Aren't they digitized?"

"Some are. This is Barkview's history in every yellowed and lovingly scribbled page." The catch in her voice reminded me of Jonathan Douglas's great-granddaughter, Jan. She'd loved this stuff too. "Families give the words of their ancestors to us for safekeeping."

More like they didn't know what to do with the stuff. It was a classic example of *can't throw it out, but no one wants it.* I didn't even know where to start.

Jennifer read my mind. She handed me two leatherbound volumes. "Peter returned these yesterday. He said both were helpful."

Whatever that meant. The reality of Jennifer's job struck me. "Do you have to carry the books upstairs when they're returned?"

"Until the dumbwaiter is repaired, yes. A group from the high school history club comes by once a week too."

That still meant Jennifer ran up and down the stairs countless times a day. No wonder she looked so fit. "Our many renovators in town aren't stepping up?" I asked.

"This is a small library. Our budget is minimal."

No excuse. Barkviewians supported their heritage. As Jennifer had said, the library was the heart of Barkview's past. "Let me see what I can do." By that I meant my aunt, of course. She'd rally the usual suspects for the good of Barkview. "Never be afraid to ask for help."

Jennifer's smile spread from ear to ear. "I knew I could count on you."

CHAPTER 5

Happy to have helped someone, I loaded G-paw into my vehicle and climbed in. No texts from either Lani or KDOG's attorney meant the chief was still questioning my sister. Legally, he had forty-eight hours before charges needed to be filed. Apparently, Uncle G intended to use every minute, which suited me just fine. No need to tell my mother about Lani until he did. Frankly, I'd choose a root canal over making that call.

Mom's words already rang in my ears. *You failed to protect your sister. You should've been watching her more closely.*

Get real. A twenty-year-old shouldn't require constant supervision. She needed to make mistakes and learn from them. Clearly, my don't-make-the-big-mistakes lecture hadn't taken. I swear I'd never been that naive. This was my mother's fault.

Lani in custody also meant that G-paw and I were a pair, but of what, exactly, I had no idea. I glanced at the wavy fluff-ball sitting at eye level on the passenger seat. Between the leash escape and his refrigerator raiding, this dog just might be as challenging as my sister to control.

Discovering Peter's killer remained my top priority. Equally as important was learning more about Skye's role in Jonathan Douglas's disappearance.

With a new focus, I headed west on Elder, turned right on First Street, and drove toward the twisty-turny, tree-lined road accessing the Terraces. Located due south from the village, the hillside homes enjoyed expansive sunset views of the Pacific, cool breezes, and privacy not often found in Southern California. Barkview's elite resided there. The higher up the hill, the more exclusive and thicker the marine layer.

Tonight proved true to form. Although it was just past dusk, I switched on my fog lights. I'd beaten my aunt to her house because she filmed her show at the studio this evening.

Peter's interest in Skye's life before 1925 intrigued me. I'd always thought she must've recorded her youth. I'd just never found another diary. Not that I'd looked too hard. Now my intuition told me to dig deeper. I just needed to figure out exactly where she would've stashed it. No better place to start than her childhood bedroom.

Russ called as the security gates slid open, admitting me to my aunt's hilltop estate. More like a peek at Tara from *Gone with the Wind* than a nod to the Victorian architecture prevalent in Barkview, the Barklay estate had been built to Celeste Barklay's specifications. Here, Greek columns and expansive lawns surrounded a three-story, whitewashed main house and carriage house now home to the Barklay Cavalier Kennel. Inside the double doors an enormous foyer, featuring a sweeping open staircase decorated with intricate plaster design work, paid tribute to a more opulent time.

I drove around the circular driveway and parked right in front. "Hi, Russ." G-paw barked before I could introduce him.

"Good evening to you, too, G-paw," Russ said.

That he knew about the dog before I'd had a chance to call him couldn't be good news. "Uncle G called you!"

"He did not. Imagine my surprise when the FBI's area director asks me to investigate a murder case involving my fiancée's sister, and I don't know a thing about it."

"I didn't want to bother you." The excuse sounded lame, even to my ears. My engagement ring weighed down my finger. We were partners. Why hadn't I called him, really?

"Consider me now bothered."

Ugh! He didn't sound mad, just disappointed again. Somehow this was going to swing right back to why I hadn't picked a wedding date yet. I just knew it. What was wrong with a long engagement anyway? It wasn't that I didn't want to marry him. I did. I just... "I'm sorry, Russ. Wait a minute. The FBI called you?"

"Yes. I'll be in Barkview in ninety minutes. Peter Gallardo was on the TSDB, the Terrorist Screening Database."

Good thing I'd parked, or I would've ended up in a ditch. My sister's boyfriend a domestic terrorist? My mother was really going to kill me now.

Before I could ask for clarification, a phone rang in the background. "That's D.C. again," Russ said. "I can't talk right now. Meet me at police headquarters. I'll fill you and the chief in on what I can."

Mr. Even Keel curt? This had to be some secret. My curiosity kicked into high gear. Suddenly, finding Skye's early diaries took on even more importance.

CHAPTER 6

Motivated, I motioned G-paw to follow me. He sort of did, taking off on a minor detour to retrieve a choice stick—a six-foot beauty encased in pale bark with a few green leaves poking out at weird angles. No tightrope walker would be caught dead with that abomination. G-paw, by contrast, carried the stick as if it were a royal scepter, his head and step both high and mighty.

I tsked as I unlocked the front door and entered. I guess I figured the dog would follow. Who knew he'd be determined to bring the double-door-size stick inside too? The crazy dog even tried to force the issue.

A clunk stopped me mid-stride on the bottom stair. I turned just as the stick *thunked* against the doorframe a second time. "G-paw!"

The dog shook his head and barreled forward again, jarring more than just his teeth. Yikes. "Turn sideways," I shouted, using hand signals. As if he could understand. Not that I wanted the stick in the house. Who knew what creatures inhabited a downed branch?

G-paw lined up with the door again. *Bang.* The stick hit the doorframe, nicking the paint. I really tried not to laugh. I attempted to bend the stick to fit through the opening, but the dog wasn't having any of it. G-paw just shook his head and tried again. *Bang.* The stick hit the doorjamb yet again.

I didn't have time for this. "Drop it."

The Golden Doodle understood my order, all right. Rebellion boiled in his chocolate-brown eyes. Memories of Ariana's German Shepherd, Gem, guarding the Shepard Diamond replayed in my mind. That dog's overprotectiveness had made me crazy, but Gem obeyed commands. G-paw did not. Well, maybe he did when it suited him.

With no time to mess around, I put my hands on my hips and finger-scolded Norman Rockwell–style. G-paw bobbed his head but finally dropped the stick on the welcome mat, effectively blocking the entry.

Score: G-paw 0, Cat 1.

I took the win and motioned the dog to follow me up the sweeping staircase to the second level. We walked together down the hall to a pretty room with a balcony overlooking the kennel and well-tended rose garden.

Although Aunt Char had redecorated the room in a welcoming, light-blue coastal motif a few years ago, I still remembered the darker hunter-green walls from my convalescence as if it were yesterday. Hard to believe the Pit Bull attack that had brought me to Barkview had been twelve years ago now. A coincidence that Aunt Char had put me in Skye's childhood room? I doubted it. I'd needed all the strength and daring I could get back then. No wonder I felt a kinship with her. I'd spent my darkest hours here with Aunt Char as my anchor.

I knelt in front of the window seat. In her later years, Skye had craved order. If she'd wanted to stash something secret, she'd have chosen a location that was easily accessible but unlikely to be investigated. I'd stored my own musings in there, shredded long ago at a "moving on" ceremony I hoped Skye hadn't practiced with her earlier diary.

G-paw's wet nose joined my hands inside the box after I lifted the lid. The scent of cedar wrapped around me as I removed a single, soft throw blanket.

I hadn't expected the location to be easy to find. I nudged G-paw aside and tapped the wood planking, methodically inspecting each board until I heard a hollow echo. Could it be this easy?

I pried at the plank's edges with my fingernails, sacrificing my French manicure in my haste. My thumbnail cracked before I reached for my phone and texted José, Barklay Kennel's manager and Aunt Char's resident handyman, to bring the appropriate tools. Sure, I could've found something to pop the boards, but José would kill me if I scratched the original wood.

José and his wife, Ria, the Barklays' longtime housekeeper, lived in a cottage adjacent to the kennel. Normally, I wouldn't bother him this late, but he'd no doubt noticed my arrival and would be checking in on me anyway. He might as well be prepared.

A few moments later, G-paw's low growl alerted me to someone's arrival. "That you, José?"

"Si, Miss Cat." Despite residing in California for the past twenty-five years, José's Guadalajaran accent remained thick. Undeterred by the Golden Doodle's reaction, he came right up the stairs. His collection of screwdrivers, crowbars, and hammers stuck out of his overalls. "We'll have that board up in no time."

No doubt. G-paw's reaction didn't surprise me either. He met the salt-and-pepper-haired man at the doorway with a chest puffed to intimidate. Funny, I never realized how big G-paw was until he just about overwhelmed the doorway. José's smile broadened as he offered the dog a stick. Not any old stick, but the branch the dog had surrendered at the door trimmed to reasonable proportions. Tail-whipping pleasure showed his feelings as he licked José's hand and took the stick in a single motion. The dog then settled by the door, gnawing.

I shook my head. José's dog-whispering skills clearly went beyond Cavaliers. "How did you know?"

José's grin took a decade off his lined face. "Retrievers like to retrieve."

"And poodles preen. When dogs are crossbred, how do you know what traits they inherit?" G-paw's tendency to take off didn't fit with either breed.

"I'll let you in on a secret."

I leaned in, ready for his pure canine wisdom. I needed all the dog-handling insight I could get. "I tripped over the branch at the front door," José smiled. "It just needed a trim."

I guess I should've thought of that. "Seriously, how do you know what a mixed breed dog's personality will be like?"

José scratched his jaw. "An educated guess, Miss Cat. Cross-breeding is designed to avoid genetic diseases and to create an animal that combines the best traits of both breeds."

"You mean it's just a roll of the dice?"

He shrugged in agreement. "Even dogs from the same litter may have different traits. Look at human siblings..."

"Lani and I are half-sisters." No reason to include us in this comparison.

"Yes, you are. Siblings, in general, may or may not even look alike. Although both parents are the same and the young-sters grow up in the same home, their personalities can differ."

Were we talking about dogs or people? I didn't want to know. Instead, I directed José's attention to the window seat. He dropped his reading glasses from the top of his head over his eyes and slipped a flat-tipped screwdriver between the wooden boards. The planks popped like a champagne cork.

My heart pounded as I shone my phone light inside. No books. Just a flash of light that led me to a dusty gold object. I wiped it on my blouse and held the nickel-size object to the light. The shape, well... I turned it a slow three hundred and sixty degrees. It kind of resembled a bird. Had it been Skye's? Some of her later aerodynamic innovations had been based on birdwatching she'd done as a preteen with her aviator brother on Barkview's bluffs. I pocketed the charm. I'd been so sure I'd find something more substantial. I was missing something. I knew it.

I must've stood there for some time because G-paw's bark startled me. José had long since left me to my thoughts, but I'd expected to be long gone by the time my aunt arrived. Yikes! If I didn't get moving, I'd miss meeting Russ.

As usual, Aunt Char swept into the room in a flash of classic St. John elegance, making me feel like something the cat dragged in. How she managed to look as fresh as the morning sun, despite putting in a long day at the mayor's office and filming her dog psychiatry show, eluded me.

G-paw bounded full speed across Skye's old room, skidding to a stop at Aunt Char's feet, his front paws airborne, while his slobbery tongue aimed right for her chin.

Two water bottles hit the floor as Aunt Char caught his paws before they snagged her knit jacket. Her face took the full-force lick. "Good to see you too, G-paw."

Ugh! Why did dogs have to lick everything? I chased down the rolling bottles while Aunt Char scratched the Golden Doodle's head.

"Anything interesting, my dear?" she asked.

"Interesting, maybe. Helpful, not so much." I held up the charm. "I need a chain."

45

Aunt Char filled a pop-up bowl for the dog. "It could be a key of some sort."

I took another long look at the birdlike shape. "To what is the question."

Aunt Char grinned. "You will figure it out, my dear."

Her confidence in me felt good. I thanked her with a smile and took a long swallow of water.

"JB told some fascinating stories about his Auntie Skye. There was one about a Venetian Carnival that would make you blush."

I doubted that. Reading about Skye's hair-raising adventures inspired me. "Where did he hear the stories?" Aunt Char's late husband had passed almost five years ago now. He would have been a child when Skye lived.

"From his father, who was Skye's younger brother. From what I understand, she left Barkview in 1925 and never returned. She was killed in a hit-and-run accident walking across the street in Dallas in 1966. Her trunk was found in a hangar at Love Field in the early 1980s and returned to Barkview. I think JB's father stashed it in the attic, thinking he'd get to it one day. Frankly, I think you're the first person to ever really go through it."

Certainly the first to read her diaries. "I guess you never know when your time is up." I'd sure faced my share of crises.

"I wish I could find her earlier diaries." I exhaled. "I can't help but believe I missed something more that she wants me to know. Something I can't explain."

"I understand. I've always felt there was more to her story." We shared a look.

If anyone understood, my aunt did—that weird, witchy thing that came over me without warning. Russ called it intuition. I had learned to trust it in my last few adventures.

"You know, the Queen Mum held a special place in Skye's heart," Aunt Char said suddenly.

Renny's however-many-greats-grandmother had been an icon. "I suppose so. Skye's photographs almost always show a Cavalier King Charles flying shotgun."

Aunt Char had an idea. I recognized that light-went-on smile right away. "Skye had an armoire in her room."

"There wasn't one there when I stayed there."

"I took it out to give you more breathing room."

That sick feeling played in my stomach. "Was it stored in the kennel?" The original Barklay Kennel, built by Celeste Barklay, had been destroyed last year in a fire that had almost taken Aunt Char. The nightmares still woke me. I fingered the charm. Most of the Barklay cast-off furniture had been stored there.

"Fortunately, the mahogany needed refinishing."

"And..." Dare I hope?

"I always felt it was important, and I sent it out for repair. It's in the attic now. Shall we take a look?" Aunt Char gestured that I lead the way,

I hugged her as I rushed past her, G-paw at my heels.

Located on the third floor, the attic was really a large unfinished room with dormer windows. That musty, grandma's attic smell struck me as G-paw brushed past me into the gloom. I felt braille-style along the wall for the light switch, my fingertips disturbing cobwebs in my hunt. Ugh! Why am I a magnet for creepy-crawly things?

Finally, I found the light switch and flicked it on. A single 100-watt bulb spread a harsh white light across the room, casting long shadows to the four corners.

I checked for spiders and then wiped the mess on my pants. All clear, I picked my way past a ghostly hat stand and stacked portraits draped in dusty once-white sheets. The last time I'd been up here, I'd found Skye's aged travel chest that had started the journey. This time, I bypassed the metal Belber wardrobe trunk covered with faded travel destination labels spanning 1927–1946. London, Paris, Venice, Egypt, New York, Rio, Hawaii, Peking, to name a few—even Orient Express rail tags—spoke to journeys made during the rise of fascism that had intrigued me.

G-paw sniffed, then sneezed, a delicate snort that made his fluffy head bob. I swallowed a chuckle at this dog's human traits as I crossed the room, beelining it to the only sheeted six-foot piece of furniture in the room. In a single swipe, I jerked the cover off, revealing an intricately carved and mirrored armoire. One side of it featured three drawers opened by flower-shaped drawer pulls, while the other had a single bar inside to hang clothing.

I took a second to appreciate the high-glossed garden scenes painstakingly carved into the wood. The empty drawers smelled of fresh cedar, no doubt thanks to the restoration. Nothing interesting there. The Golden Doodle squeezed by me and sat inside the silk-wallpapered hanging closet. I shooed him out to better investigate every corner and planked floor. Nothing there either. Had the restorer covered a hiding place with the freshly-applied wallpapered backing?

"There's nothing here." Frustration snuck through my announcement.

"Let's think about this." Aunt Char stepped back and surveyed the piece with a critical eye. She tiptoed closer and ran her finger along the upper arch.

"You know, people were much shorter in 1900. I believe Celeste Barklay was barely five feet tall."

The *duh* moment hit. "And if you wanted to hide some-thing from your mother..." I pulled a dust cover off the closest chair and dragged it to the armoire.

Aunt Char held the chair steady as I climbed up. No argument from me. All I needed was for another aftershock to hit and I'd end up on the floor.

Up close, I realized the two-inch floral molding capping the armoire depicted roses. I inspected each flower. Nothing odd or telling. They all appeared to be perfect.

I stepped down, moved the chair to the right side, and climbed up to continue my search. As I rounded the front corner, something clicked. At least, I thought it did. It happened so quickly, wishful thinking may have prevailed.

Aunt Char heard it too. I could tell from her satisfied grin. I climbed down and moved the chair closer to the corner for a more direct look. I pressed the wood again. This time the molding swung outward, revealing a cubby just big enough for a book or two. I shone the light inside and slid out two aged, once-white, cracked leather-bound books, one cover plain and the other painted with a red rose. Was this the smoking gun, or would the information contained in the book exonerate Skye from wrongdoing? Did I really want to know? Deniability wasn't always a bad defense. Whatever I found must be turned over to the Hall of Fame selection committee.

Trepidation stirred. Right now, the evidence against Skye amounted to a highly suspect he-said-she-said accusation, which might or might not even influence the group. The information in this diary could end Skye's chances at aviation recognition or prove her worthiness once and for all. I had no choice but to look. The truth must be told.

I opened the plain book first. It looked like a logbook of sorts. At least, that's what the longitude and latitude numbers indicated.

I held my breath as I opened the decorated book and read the first page.

Property of Elizabeth Rose Barklay. Keep your nosey, sticky fingers off this Journal unless you want them cut off with a dull paring knife and fed to the sharks.

G-paw's bark said it all.
I read the first entry.

June 5, 1921
I am not a writer. No matter what mother says, nothing important or extraordinary will ever happen to me in Barkview, the most boring place in America.

Little did sixteen-year-old Skye know.

I skipped through the lined pages crammed with a familiar elegant script to the last entry: June 25, 1925. Four days before Jonathan Douglas's disappearance. The book I'd found in Skye's travel case had begun in 1927. What happened in the missing two years? There had to be another journal.

CHAPTER 7

Much as I wanted to continue reading, I wisely chose domestic harmony. Skye's adventures would have to wait. I motioned G-paw to follow me. Time to learn what secrets Russ had uncovered.

I tested my Jag's handling on Rock Road as I white-knuckled it through the fog. I'd never hear the end of being late. Fortunately, I spotted Russ's Land Rover as I turned left on 5th Street and followed him into the parking lot. One of the few all-brick structures in town, police headquarters stood out in a town filled with airy, gingerbread-trimmed Victorians and iconic mansard roofs. That the building remained standing after the many earthquakes in its seventy-year history had to be a testament to its enduring strength and service to the community.

G-paw cocked his head and stared as tall, dark, and insanely handsome Russ opened my car door and leaned in for a kiss. The Golden Doodle had other ideas. Instead of waiting for the passenger side door to open, the dog leaped across the driver's seat, separating Russ and me in a flash of honey-colored fluff.

Russ caught the dog by the collar, halting his flight and bringing G-paw to a perfect heel. "Mind your manners. She's mine."

The dog's oh-so-cute head toss almost worked. Was G-paw staking a claim on me? Caught between shock and laughter, I sputtered, "Y-you both need to relax."

Was that a game-on challenge between Russ and G-paw? Me, coveted by a dog? I couldn't begin to process that concept, but I did scratch G-paw's head and coquettishly trace Russ's clean-shaven jaw with my forefinger. "This way, boys."

They followed, bumping each other in their haste. Flanked by deputy dogs Max and Maxine, Uncle G met us at the door, his signature toothpick twirling in his mouth. The bend in his rolled-up cuffs spoke of too many hours since he'd reported in this morning.

"This better be good," he growled and motioned the three of us to follow him around the granite information counter to his glass-walled office. As Russ stepped aside to allow me and G-paw to precede him, another aftershock sent a groan and shimmy through the building. Russ steadied me as I reached for the doorframe.

A shriek and shattering ceramic originating from one of the cubicles affected my pulse rate. Uncle G's furrowed brows looked like a prayer for patience.

"You okay?" Russ's hand at the small of my back helped. I always felt safe with him nearby.

I nodded. "I'm not really spooked, just on edge." The shake's intensity felt equal to the last quake. Was a stronger one still coming? "Same thing in LA?"

"Not as intense. The epicenter is on the Rose Canyon fault in San Diego County."

Another reference to a rose? Was Skye trying to tell me something?

Uncle G sat down behind his smoked-glass desk. Autographed photos of two previous presidents shaking his hand hung on the gray wall behind him, a testament to a career well spent. A fancy plasma TV screen overwhelmed the other.

G-paw shrugged off the German Shepherds' intimidating once-over and high-stepped it between Russ and me. The Golden Doodle's casual confidence impressed me. While my aunt's Cavalier took over every room she entered, G-paw just fit in.

Russ wasted no time on pleasantries and immediately displayed his computer data on the plasma screen for all of us to see.

"Before coming to Barkview," Russ announced, "Peter Gallardo was involved with HDB, a conservation group protesting the hazardous effects of dams on biodiversity. Four of his colleagues are currently serving time in federal prison, charged with domestic terrorism for planting a bomb at a Texas hydroelectric plant. Peter was questioned but not charged."

No way the geeky, self-absorbed academic was a real terrorist. Uncle G's toothpick snapped. Like me, he couldn't believe it either. Was Peter hiding in Barkview, or was he here for a more nefarious reason? "How did Peter escape prosecution?"

"His family owns Cielo Azul Distilleries," Russ replied.

"The blue-bottled tequila and rum manufacturers?" What wasn't to like about their pineapple-infused tequila?

"Among other international brands. The company was founded in the late 1940s. It remains privately held today."

A photo of a distinguished gentleman with salt-and-pepper hair dominated the plasma screen. "Peter's grandfather?" The family resemblance was uncanny.

Russ nodded. "Peter's two older sisters both have Harvard MBAs and run the company. Peter's mother owns and operates Sipper Doodle Drinks." A picture of the recognizable Doodled cans with the patented spout popped on the screen. Russ confirmed Lani's information on the company.

"Did you find Peter's Doodler?" I asked.

Uncle G shook his head. "We checked both his house and his office."

I had too. No reason to admit that just yet. I felt Russ's gaze boring into me and blushed. I swear that man knew exactly when I skirted the whole truth. "What was Peter's cause of death?" I had to divert Russ's scrutiny from me lest I admit far more than necessary.

"Officially, he drowned, but it appears he had a heart attack. We are waiting for toxicology before finalizing."

"Why? Peter had a heart arrhythmia. He treated it with"—I remembered Lani's explanation—"digoxin."

My heart about skipped a beat as Uncle G sat upright. "You think Peter's death is a homicide?" I asked, but it wasn't really a question. I saw confirmation in both men's eyes. "Did you match Lani's DNA to the coffee cup lipstick?"

"Not yet."

"So she's free to go?"

"Your sister's"—that Uncle G emphasized the relationship didn't bode well—"fingerprints are at the crime scene and Peter's home."

"She's explained both."

"Not the cash payments."

"Cash?" That made no sense. I paid Lani's living expenses, from tuition to room and board and a generous stipend. She had no need for money from Peter.

"Peter's financials show Venmo payments amounting to over a thousand dollars a month going to Lani," Uncle G explained.

"She walks G-paw." The dog nodded his head, seemingly in agreement. "Three times a day times thirty days adds up." I thought I recovered fast enough.

Uncle G's frown deepened. He'd found something else I wasn't going to like.

"Lani's DNA is on a toothbrush in Peter's bathroom."

"So? They were"—I cleared my throat—"dating." Had it been more? Russ didn't even have a toothbrush at my house.

"Evidence supports Peter being killed in a jealous rage."

"Please. Lani releases flies." And lizards and spiders... Ick.

No arguments, just Uncle G's Rock of Gibraltar stance. "Until I know more, Lani stays here."

I needed to find the elusive lipstick donor. "What about finding the Doodler?"

"I'll send divers down in the lagoon in the morning to look around," the chief announced.

"Care for some company?" Russ asked.

Uncle G's agreement didn't surprise me. Neither did Russ's gesture for me to take my leave. More was going on here than either of them would say with me in the room. I bit back my frustration. I hated this "need to know" world Russ lived in. My sister was the prime suspect here. I had a right to know.

I took my cue and yawned. "I'm beat. I'll see you in the morning."

Russ held the door for me. "Meet me at Sea Dog Dive Shop at 7 a.m."

I nodded. No way I'd miss looking around the lagoon after my earlier chat with Jennifer. Could there really be homes and caves underwater there? I hadn't been surprised when I'd learned Russ was a certified diver. The man did everything well. It had been years since I'd put on a wetsuit and dived in the cold Pacific, but if Jennifer was right and Peter had been searching in patterns, he hadn't only been studying starfish. He'd been looking for something. Something that could've gotten him killed.

CHAPTER 8

My date with Skye's diary took longer to get started than anticipated. I swear G-paw sniffed every corner in my townhouse, including every shoe in my closet. Are my feet really that sweet smelling? If that wasn't weird enough, he sat directly in front of my refrigerator and eyed it until I broke down and opened the door for his exploration.

And look he did. Every item. On every shelf, including on the door. My grand plan to protect my favorite snacks went south when he stood on his hind legs and pawed the peanut butter jar right off the top shelf. The plastic jar bounced on the tile and rolled across the floor. I could only stare as he secured the jar with one paw and twisted off the lid with the other. How was that even possible? So much for needing the massive bag of dry dog food that Sandy had dropped off. The Golden Doodle preferred the junk variety.

I guess I should've reprimanded him. Even I knew boundaries governed the human-canine relationship. But I nearly busted a gut watching his head bob like a bouncing ball while his tongue stretched out for that last blob of peanut butter on the tip of his nose. I mean, what wasn't to like about a truly self-reliant clown? He even nosed his way out the sliding glass door to do his business and closed it on his return. Was the stick he dropped at my feet an offering or a hint to play? I wasn't sure, but there was no way I'd throw that thing indoors, and it was overcast-dark outside.

I scratched the dog's head instead. Stick primarily in his mouth, G-paw just about purred, then flopped down at my feet and closed his eyes. I replaced my worse-for-wear pants and blouse with leopard-print pajamas, found a sturdy gold box-chain for Skye's charm, and slipped it around my neck. Frankly, the whole scene looked very Midwest Americana. I grabbed my shiraz du jour, made a turkey sandwich, and settled into the broken-in corner of the sectional lounge, anxious to read Skye's words.

The dog had another plan. He nudged me with the stick as he climbed on top of me, all sixty pounds of him pressed into my lap.

"G-paw. Down." I spat caramel-colored hair out of my mouth. Ugh! A fifteen-pound Cavalier made a reasonable lap dog. Not a massive Golden Doodle. I pushed the dog off my lap, only to have him plop his head on my shoulder.

Enough. More firmly, I said, "G-paw, down." He heard me. I saw yearning in his dark eyes. Suddenly, his front paws wrapped around my neck like a furry scarf, his fluffy hair tickling my nose. Great. Now, I was blanketed in a toasty Golden Doodle. The warmth felt good—great, really—but I couldn't breathe. I dropped the book and tried to push him off my chest. No amount of shoving moved him.

Like every other exhausted parent, I finally resorted to bribery to get my way. I traded half of my sandwich. G-paw inhaled it and settled on the sofa beside me, his chin comfortably resting in my lap with goal-achieved finality.

Score: G-paw 1, Cat 1. I seriously had to fix this in the morning.

Finally settled, I opened Skye's diary and started reading. Fortunately, her penmanship proved easy to decipher, despite her period slang, as I meandered through what amounted to the wandering musings of a teenager, trying to find herself with one foot in the Victorian era and the other reaching for the freedom experienced during the Great War. She wrote about her older brother, Harrington (Harry), who'd been killed in a dogfight back in 1918; Victoria (Tory) Rose, the future Queen Mum Barklay Cavalier; her best friend Edna Oldeman; and her rocky relationship with her out-of-touch mother. Nothing earth-shattering. In fact, I started dozing until the entry for June 26, 1922, woke me up.

> *A Curtiss Model R Floatplane landed right on the water and vanished. Tory Rose and I saw it from the bluff. I thought it a mirage until the dog pulled me down the embankment. I had to sneak her into the bath before Mother saw her filthy feet. Thank goodness I'd worn breeches (Mother would die) since I slid down on my bottom. We found nothing. The plane disappeared in the cliffs. It had a Curtiss V-X engine. I'd read all about the new advances. 160 hp. Faster than a condor. Harry would've taught me to fly. No matter what Mother said. I don't care if women don't fly aeroplanes. Why not? I am smarter than the suitors she brings to me.*

Where was this place, exactly? The lagoon didn't have high rock walls. Did it a hundred years ago, before the dam changed the water patterns and flooded the area?

If so, what size cave would be needed to house an airplane? I googled the specifications: forty-five feet wide and twenty-four feet long. Even the model with fold-up wings required a minimum of thirty feet.

I continued reading.

June 27, 1922
I told Mother I wanted to visit Edna. I listened when she lectured me why marrying was better than becoming a companion to a harridan like the widow, Sally Tomlinson. Poor Edna. Jonathan Douglas broke her heart when he'd come home from the Great War and married the French seamstress, Marie Le Bonne. Edna refused to marry anyone else. Tory Rose and I drove the baby blue Buick 21-44 roadster back to the lagoon. I know Mother bought it for Tory Rose. She looks so regal riding in the passenger seat. I am just her chauffeur. We hid on the beach behind a boulder and waited. No floatplane arrived. I had tea with Edna and asked her about the seaplane. Living at Mrs. Tomlinson's, she can see both the Barkview cliffs and the lagoon. She must've seen it too.

That house again, located on a land spit with a view of both water bodies. Was it the missing clue to locating Jonathan's secret beach and cave?

June 24, 1922
I overheard the servants gossiping about liquor arriving tonight. It made sense that the rumrunners delivered on moonless nights. Early this morning, Tory Rose and I hid behind the same boulder and waited. Did the pilot work for the rumrunners? Was the plane used to smuggle or just as a lookout? That sleek body couldn't hold much.

I heard the V-X engine before I saw the floatplane clear the fog bank and gracefully dip into the water on the north shore. I watched the aeroplane disappear into the brush. There has to be a cave there big enough to hide it. My heart pounded as I crept closer. I saw him then, the cat's pajamas. The most cheeky tall, dark, and handsome man (clean-shaven except for a dashing dark mustache). He smiled when he saw me and bowed like a continental gentleman. "Mi Cielo, your servant." Tory liked him too. She sniffed his feet and offered her head to be scratched.

His name is Crack. He flew with Pancho Villa for Mexican independence and shot down Germans in the Great War. He works for Jonathan Douglas now and gave me the Red Door's password. Mother would be displeased if she knew. She can't stop me. I am eighteen.

Crack mixed me a Gin Ricky just like they serve at Agua Caliente in Tijuana. It tickled my nose. I felt free. Why do they call the speakeasy the Red Door? The door isn't red. The dance club is below Doc Turner's. We talked about my brother and how we watched the eagles soar together. Crack promised to take me flying in his Model R seaplane. I met Jonathon and Marie. They are so in love. Edna never had a chance.

Today, a posh grooming salon primped Barkview's canines in the downstairs rooms of that same building. What remained of the speakeasy, and who was Edna Oldeman? Had history forgotten her?

I glanced at G-paw snoring at my side as my wall clock bonged eleven times. I dialed Sandy. It wasn't too late. By her own admission, she never slept anyway, primarily due to her Jack Russell Terrier.

"What's up, Boss? You hardly ever call this late." Sandy

sounded more breathless than actually tired. To be that young again...

"Nothing. I mean, I found Skye's teenage diary in her old armoire."

"Yeah! You've proven she didn't kill Jonathan, right?"

I hated to disappoint her. "Not exactly. The last entry is June 25, 1925."

"There's another book."

Sandy's announcement depressed me. Finding yet another diary wouldn't be easy. I had no idea where to look for it.

"What do you need me to do?" Sandy asked, always ready to help.

I liked that about her. "I'm scuba diving in the lagoon with Russ at 7 a.m."

Sandy's phone clanked on a hard surface.

"Come on, it's not that early." Okay, I admit, I'm not a morning person. I proudly wear my cranky pants until I've inhaled my first cup of coffee or three.

"I'll come by at 6:30 with your Woofing Best coffee..."

I smiled. She knew me too well. "That's okay. I'm sure Russ will bring it."

Her chuckle warmed me. "Oh yeah! He's got you figured out. So, what else do you need?"

"Skye had a friend named Edna Oldeman. She must have been a relative of Will's." The oldest employee of the Old Barkview Inn, Will still operated the hotel's restored Otis elevator.

"That makes sense. His family built the hotel in 1890." I recognized keyboard clicks in the background. "It wasn't until 1932 that the Great Depression drastically reduced tourism and forced an ownership change. Did you know the fortunes of four of the five founding Barkview families reversed by 1934? Only the Barklays' wealth remained."

I knew all that. I heard Sandy typing in the background. "According to this, Edna caused quite the family rift when she refused to marry her cousin because she was in love with Jonathan," she explained. "Geez. This is interesting. The Old Barkview Inn underwent a renovation in the mid-1920s that contributed to the Oldemans losing the hotel after the 1929 crash. Had Edna married her cousin, her dowry would've stopped them from going into debt. After Jonathan's disappearance, she was engaged to marry a Chicago hotelier. I found the engagement announcement and the wedding menu. Nothing easily accessible on the genealogy search, though."

"You mean there's no branch to follow?" Sandy and her computer tracked information better than an encyclopedia.

"Exactly. It's odd. Edna just sort of vanishes. I can't even find a record of her married name."

"Jonathan's death changed a lot of lives. Maybe Edna just moved on too. She was Skye's best friend. I can't help but think Skye wanted us to learn about her."

Sandy responded with feverish typing again. "I'll dig deeper."

Good thing Sandy loved to hunt for impossible information. I had more. "It might be nothing, but Skye talks about a pilot named Crack. He flew for Pancho Villa and in World War I."

"You think this guy is important, don't you?"

"I do." Don't ask me why. I just did.

"No last name? What about a nationality? World War I involved twenty countries who contributed pilots. Was he Mexican?"

Ugh! "Maybe. Pancho Villa was the president of Mexico. I know it's not much to go on."

More keystrokes in the background. "Hmm. 'Crack' was a term associated with ace pilots. Let's see, a flying ace was defined as a military aviator credited with shooting down five or more enemy aircraft during aerial combat. Geez. There are like a hundred from the United States alone. Cross-referenced with those of Mexican descent, there are three."

"Pancho Villa was assassinated in 1923. Crack could've just been any random World War I pilot who became a mercenary for Mexico." Don't ask me how I came up with that. Must've been from a movie.

"True. But the person who ratted out Jonathan was supposedly deported. A Mexican pilot makes sense. Especially if the pilot was the lookout."

No argument from me.

"I'm not really sure if Peter was looking for the Douglas Diamond or not," Sandy continued. "The dam project on Peter's computer involved an environmental group called..."

"HDB," I said. Maybe Russ was right about the connection.

"Yes. How did you...? Never mind, Russ must've told you. My point is, Peter has data showing the overflow from the Rose Canyon Dam project may be causing the sea star wasting syndrome that is killing the area's starfish population."

"OMG!" Talk about a bomb. Potential catastrophic consequences from an economically sound eighty-year-old dam project? Could this be motive to kill Peter?

"No kidding. The list of folks who'd want to bury this information is long and powerful. I'll try to limit the suspects. We need to find Peter's Doodler. He references a specific starfish he supposedly has a drawing of that I can't identify," Sandy said.

I scratched G-paw's fluffy head. "I'll keep an eye out for the red neck strap." How hard could it be to find? "Issue will be if it's a sandy or rocky bottom in the lagoon." Had Peter really only been looking for that starfish and not the lost treasure? "Did you find out anything more on who owns the land?"

"Current owners are a Delaware trust. I haven't found the

principals yet. The original deed's dated 1897. George Tomlinson purchased all the land surrounding the lagoon. The family members were fishermen. Around 1900, George's brother opened a canning operation that the family continued to supply with tuna."

"I know the Tomlinsons went to San Pedro after they left Barkview in 1925," I said. "Any idea where they are today?"

"No. I found a record of George Tomlinson II selling tuna to a San Pedro cannery in 1929. Nothing after that. I'll follow the genealogy trail," Sandy said. "I did compare the 1911 and current topographical charts." Annoyance laced her tone, the self-inflicted kind. "I missed it. Pure and simple."

"We all did. We were all so focused on the ocean cliffs." Could the location explain why the Douglas Diamond remained lost for so long?

"No excuses. This just might be the breakthrough we've been looking for."

"Or just another rabbit hole. Finding a lost cave potentially closed off by an earthquake underwater is a statistical longshot."

"Perhaps. But the prophecy is on our side," Sandy insisted.

I had to love her optimism. Call me a skeptic, but a prophecy told by the resident psychic, who happened to have a personal agenda, could hardly be considered a reliable source.

Sandy repeated the words long-committed to memory. "'The bear will fall to peasant rule and rise again in the one-hundredth-and-twentieth year, when the golden suns unite to revive what was once stolen from the soul of the true leader.'"

"If you believe the words apply to the Douglas Diamond and the timeline Madame Orr laid out," I said.

"I know we only have Madame Orr's word that this year is the one-hundred-and-twentieth year referenced, but Victor Roma did offer a million-dollar finder's fee."

"That he doesn't pay out if the stone isn't found," I had to add. "Politically, Russia's leadership is vulnerable now. Victor sees an opportunity, but his plans rely on the Douglas Diamond being found."

"What is your intuition saying?" Sandy asked point-blank.

As if that information mattered. "That we're closer."

Hope crept back into Sandy's voice. "It is curious that a woman from the same time period is directing us."

No denying that. Was that Skye's goal? Or the goal of the person trying to discredit her? How did Peter and his environmental history fit into all this? After my scuba dive with Russ, it would be time to visit Madame Orr.

CHAPTER 9

I must've slept through my ringing alarm, because G-paw's sharp, get-up bark penetrated my consciousness just as the wall clock bonged seven times. Ugh! I shot to my feet. Totally disoriented, I stumbled over a lump at my feet and hit the floor with a *thunk*.

I'd fallen asleep on the couch. No wonder my back felt like a twisted pretzel. I yawned. Maybe I shouldn't have read Skye's diary until 3 a.m. I couldn't remember any of it anyway.

G-paw greeted me with a slobbery kiss smack on the lips. What a way to start the morning. I stumbled into the bathroom, intent on brushing the socks off my teeth and decontaminating.

I traded my PJs for a functional one-piece bathing suit beneath black sweats and a bulky KDOG sweatshirt and brushed my teeth in a record seven minutes and thirty-six seconds. No time to feed my caffeine fix. I was already late!

I tripped over a cheese tub dead center on the kitchen floor. G-paw had helped himself to breakfast with no mess. Good. The jalapeño cheddar spread hadn't been my favorite anyway.

The dog had even licked the container clean. No need to walk him either; the pile right outside the patio door, next to that coveted stick, said it all. No doubt the dog had done this all before.

The Golden Doodle even led me to the garage door. Once outside, he pushed by me to leap into the car. Ugh! A morning dog. At least one of us had their sights on adventure. I called Russ as I drove the two-mile stretch from my Shores townhouse to the Sea Dog Dive Shop.

"I'm sorry. I just left the house," I said.

"Good morning to you too." Russ's upbeat tone chafed.

I bit my tongue. Any comment on four hours of sleep wasn't going to come out right.

Russ continued, "I have scuba tanks in my car and a 5-mil wetsuit for you. Water temperature is sixty-two degrees. Meet me on the southeast beach entry off First Street." The beep in the background indicated another call. "I have to go."

He disconnected before I could agree. Curiosity bubbled inside me. If this was related to Peter's case, it would be pointless to ask questions. Russ never broke protocol. He'd never tell me anyway. My head pounded. The secrecy really made me crazy, even though I knew it was part of his job. I glanced at the engagement ring on my hand. Was I really ready to sign up for this for life? There had to be more to it than a simple murder for him to be this involved.

I parked in front of the Sea Dog Dive Shop. Knowing Russ, he'd chosen too small a size wetsuit for me, which I wasn't in any mood to shimmy into at this hour.

Located on the east side of First Street among a grouping of 1920s craftsman beach bungalows separated by vibrant butterfly gardens, the green-trimmed building faced the foggy Pacific. Its colorful past included serving as an early-warning radar station during World War II and a surfers' hostel in the

1960s and 1970s. Five years ago, Jordan Thompson had moseyed into Barkview with a camera around his neck and Baxter, his chocolate lab, at his feet. The two never left. Jordan insisted the decision had been mutual, but most Barkviewians believed Baxter had plopped his butt in the sand and refused to return to Denver. Over the years, Jordan honed his photography skills to include award-winning oceanographic videography.

G-paw exited the car first, again, and bounded up the path. He jumped paws-to-shoulders on the shaggy-haired, beach-blond surfer blocking the screened entry. I followed more slowly, my wry smile in full view as the Golden Doodle lavished licks on Jordan's scruffy beard and brows while he balanced a Woofing Best coffee cup.

"Russ said not to let you inside until you've had this." Jordan's hand quivered as he handed it to me.

I bit back a snarky comment, instead lacing my fingers around the warm paper cup. The whiff of caramel cappuccino felt like a familiar hug. My first long swallow tempered my growl. I leaned against the doorframe and looked out over the sand. It was too early to see the surf through the morning fog, but I did hear it rolling onto shore.

And this was why I was going to figure out how to deal with Russ's secrecy and marry him. The man just got me.

I watched a butterfly flutter around the garden beside me and enjoyed another coffee swallow before smiling at Jordan. "Thank you. I needed that."

Jordan shoved his hands into the pockets of his board shorts. "Whew! Remind me to schedule our appointments for after nine."

"A sound plan. What happened to your flowers?" Small, recently planted flowers filled the front edge. It looked odd compared to the rest of the shin-high display.

"An animal must've gotten into the flower bed on Monday night. The whole front section was trampled when I came in on Tuesday. I replanted last night."

That had to be a pain. G-paw preceded me through the door Jordan now held open. The vibrant underwater photography lining the walls captured my attention. From spirited harbor seals and breaching gray whales to colorful garibaldis swaying amid giant kelp, each poster-sized photo made underwater Barkview real.

The dog surveyed the room with one long airborne sniff and then sat at my side. Jordan's voice caught as he scratched G-paw's head. "Baxter would've liked you."

I didn't know what to say. Jordan's dog had crossed the rainbow bridge some time ago. Odd he hadn't brought home a new friend yet. Jordan's wistful head shake turned serious. "Please pass my sympathy to your sister. Poor kid. She and Peter were good together."

I froze. Was I the last to know Lani and Peter had been plus-ones or just blind? "You know Lani?"

"Of course. She came in a few times a week to pick up and return Peter's tanks for him."

My helpless sister? "Lani carried tanks?"

"Oh no. My momma taught me better. When I was here, I loaded the tanks into her car." I could see Lani enjoying the view of Jordan's muscular frame at work. "Lani always took a beach wagon." Jordan pointed to a soft-sided blue wagon with holders for six tanks.

The same wagon we'd found at the crime scene. Did Lani really have opportunity and means? "Did Lani pick up tanks yesterday?"

"I don't know. She sent a text ordering them on Monday." Jordon showed me his phone.

Sure enough, Lani's number showed on the screen. Lani, planning in advance? She could barely get to class on time.

Jordan continued, "I left the wagon with two tanks out back."

"Did Peter normally order two tanks?"

"Most of the time. Lani did occasionally dive with Peter. I didn't think anything of it since Lani texted in the order."

"You didn't see her?" No cameras in Barkview meant no confirmation either way.

He shook his head. "I took some tourists on a sunrise dive at the Barkview Cliffs yesterday. The wagon was still here when I left."

That confirmed the librarian, Jennifer's, statement that Peter had arrived around eight. "How did Peter pay you?"

"I charged his credit card on Fridays. It was easier. He liked to pick up before I arrived in the morning and usually returned when I was out on a day dive trip."

"When Peter ordered tanks, were they all returned empty?"

"Every time. In fact, I planned to talk to him about it. He sucked them dry."

Could Peter just have lost track of time in the water and accidentally drowned? "That's not good."

"You're a certified diver. You know the rules."

I did.

"I planned to talk to Peter about it. That's just irresponsible, not paying attention to your air supply." Jordan noted my frown. "Do you know if Peter found the cause of the SSWS?"

"He spoke to you about it?"

"I dive in the area a lot," Jordan explained. "He was looking for a specific sea star. I'd never seen anything like it before. Peter showed me a picture of it he'd drawn on his Doodler. He said he'd seen one in the lagoon. He wanted to know if I'd seen it anywhere else."

That made sense. "What did it look like?"

"A three-pronged thing. I can't even draw stick figures. My talent is in photography. Peter had a detailed drawing on his Doodler."

Another reason to find that Doodler.

"Chad Williams asked me about it too," Jordan added.

"The *Finders Keepers* blogger?"

Jordan nodded. "Chad told me Peter showed him the picture. He wanted to know if Peter was for real."

Now that sounded like the egomaniac hunting for the Douglas Diamond. "What did you tell him?"

"Same as I told Peter. I'd never seen anything like it before. Chad wanted to know about my lagoon dives."

"You dive in the lagoon?" Was I the only person who'd never considered it?

"Only to do some checkout dives." A certified instructor, Jordan offered Open Water and resort certifications. "Over by the south side entrance. It's mostly a sandy bottom and not too scary to practice clearing a flooded mask."

I'd hated that part of the test. "Have you seen any caves there?"

"Nothing that looked interesting enough to explore. The guy I bought the dive shop from told me about some old buildings on the east side, but I haven't looked for them. I can't imagine anything is left after the dam project flooded them back in 1930-something. The elements would have taken their toll by now. Diving by the Barkview cliffs makes more sense, especially for the tourists. I've intended to try the back side of Bark Rock, but the current never seems to be favorable."

Exactly why paddleboarding there didn't appeal to me either. I'd never live down calling the Coast Guard for a rescue less than a mile off the coast.

"Where is Chad exploring nowadays?" I asked.

"As far as I know, the same caves as everyone else," Jordan said.

"Anyone else diving regularly?"

Jordan chuckled. "Every wannabe treasurer hunter. Victor Roma's reward has helped my business."

I leaned in to whisper, "Any gossip about the treasure?"

"Everyone is tight-lipped around me. Afraid I'd steal their thunder, I guess." Jordan scratched his bearded jaw.

"You mean you're not looking?" Wasn't everyone? A million-dollar finder's fee with no questions asked...

"I'm a simple man."

With expensive tastes, if the first-class video equipment around the shop meant anything. The gleam in his blue eyes screamed lotto-fever too. Nothing wrong with dreaming, but his protest made me wonder. "Where do you think the treasure is?"

"Long buried in the hillside." As if to prove his point, an aftershock rippled through the building, rattling the metal scuba tanks and pegged regulators.

Did I really want to do any cave diving today? Why take a chance of suffering Jonathan's fate?

CHAPTER 10

I parked in the popular surfers' parking lot beside Russ's Land Rover. As expected, we weren't alone. A half-dozen vehicles filled the packed dirt lot. Three were equipped with bike racks. Two had capacious surfboard racks, and one a Surf Dog on Board bumper sticker. To G-paw's annoyance, I snapped photos of the license plates before opening the door. His seat pacing seemed more caged-tiger-frustrated than potty-related. The Golden Doodle confirmed my opinion when I finally did open the passenger door. He leaped out and darted right down the trail, barking all the way to the beach from the sound of it, scattering seagulls and announcing our arrival.

So much for seaside serenity. I looped my regulator and dive computer octopus over my shoulder, glad I'd packed it last night. I followed the dog's paw prints to Russ's equipment stash on the beach.

Dressed in black, neoprene, Farmer John wetsuit bottoms, Russ studied the bluffs through high-powered binoculars. With one hand resting on G-paw's head and his feet firmly planted beneath him, he looked so much like an ancient mariner riding out a squall, I blinked. What I'd read in Skye's diary and reality seemed to be blurring.

"What are you looking for?" I squinted, trying to make out his line of sight.

Russ acknowledged me with a wave, not interrupting his focus until I kissed his neck. "Point of reference," he said.

Whatever that meant. "Thank you for the coffee. I needed it."

"No kidding." His forefinger brushed my cheek. His scrutiny changed to the surrounding landscape.

"Anyone out there?"

"No one I'm not aware of."

Spoken like a true spy. Translated, his folks were watching us. Frustration stirred. This wasn't a murder of passion. I could feel it. Yet my sister sat in jail.

"What did you find in Skye's diary?" Russ asked.

"Nothing to exonerate her from murder or theft allegations."

"You didn't expect to." No question in his statement. His matter-of-factness refocused me.

"I'm not giving up. There is always a clue."

"You just need to know where to look," we said in unison.

I felt better. He always knew how to do that. "Why are we here? The Doodler is more likely near the murder scene."

"The chief and his divers are searching that area," Russ replied.

Which freed us up to search elsewhere. "You found the location of the widow, Sally Tomlinson's, lagoon view home?" I asked.

"Ah. She is awake." I had his full attention now as he kissed my nose.

If I hadn't been at that point, his touch did it. I said the first thing that came to mind. "Chad talked to Jordan about Peter's hunt for the sea star wasting syndrome."

"He viewed Peter as a rival?" asked Russ.

We definitely thought alike. "I don't know. Chad considers the Douglas Diamond to be his personal treasure. I imagine he has already spent the reward."

"Killing Peter doesn't track. Added scrutiny could jeopardize the search."

"You don't think it was an accident?" He knew something. I could tell.

"Toxicology came back. Peter had high levels of Digoxin in his blood," said Russ. "He overdosed on his heart arrhythmia pills?" My heart sank. It was the same prescription Sandy and I had found in the front seat of Lani's car. She'd had undeniable opportunity. Not telling could be considered obstruction, but there was no way I'd give up on my sister.

"Not exactly. Officially, he drowned in a diving accident. The excessive amount of Digoxin would cause confusion, fast heartbeat, vision changes, and color changes..."

"He didn't know which way was up." What a frightening way to go.

"Probably not. My gut is telling me the killer knew exactly what he was doing. We found traces of the drug in the Sipper Doodle can G-paw found under the bush."

"The can with the spout?" Peter had been Doodled to death.

Russ nodded.

A piece to this crazy puzzle slipped into place. "The cans in cup holders at the beach were a setup. Peter never drank without the Sipper Doodle spout."

Russ didn't argue. "I'd say the assailant knew Peter well."

Which didn't help Lani's case any. I had to ask. "You spoke to Lani, right? Did she know what the drug did?"

"No."

No hesitation. He'd believed her. I exhaled in a rush, more relieved than I cared to admit. I'd believed in Lani's innocence all along—convincing Uncle G remained to be seen.

"Let's see if we can find the house and cave." Russ handed me a pair of well-worn nude pantyhose.

I held them gingerly. "Do I want to know?"

"Definitely not."

What he said didn't matter as much as how he'd said it.

"Hey. Better than neoprene knuckle burn or too large a wetsuit," he added too quickly.

My frown turned into a smile. He'd had the foresight to plan ahead. I gave in as gracefully as anyone squiggling on someone else's pantyhose with a Golden Doodle swatting at the dangling feet. After that battle, the larger wetsuit slipped on with only a single broken nail.

Russ helped me into my BCD and tank. I added the weights to counter the wetsuit's buoyancy. A quick double check on my dive computer and gauges, and I was ready. Like emperor penguins, we waddled across the sand. What a picture.

I filled my BC with air and walked in. The ice-cold water took the breath right out of me. Okay, sixty-two degrees wasn't freezing, but with the sun still playing hide-and-seek behind the low clouds, the air temperature barely matched the water and wasn't helping any either.

I missed diving in Hawaii.

Floating on the surface, I faced the brush-dotted bluff. A hundred years ago, Skye had stood near here and watched a seaplane land in this lagoon. Where had it gone?

If the plane came in from the west, the cave had to be on the southeast side of the lagoon.

Russ gave me the descend signal, and I bled the BCD's air. Thanks to my weight belt, I slowly sank into the murky water.

G-paw just lay on the beach with one eye on the water and the other on the entry path. A Golden Doodle watchdog? He'd lick you to death. I did know that he'd be right there when we returned.

I switched on my dive light, illuminating the twigs and tree bark suspended around me as I sank into the water. We equalized on the sandy bottom before I checked my compass and pointed east. Russ didn't argue. Not that he could underwater. The only sound was my own meditative inhale and exhale. As we swam, the bottom changed from sand interspersed with small rock piles to more sizable boulders, leading finally to a pile of rubble of what could be loosely described as an ancient dwelling. Could this be the remains of Sally Tomlinson's home?

Russ swam past the relics toward a natural rock wall. Forty feet underwater today, in 1922 it had most likely been at sea level. We ascended to twenty feet, where the rocks leveled into a flat surface. Could this be the bluff where Skye had waited for the floatplane?

Russ flutter-kicked across the level area and then dipped down the wall, shining his light on the rocks. Encrusted with a large variety of invertebrates that included camouflaged sea stars, sand dollars, and sea cucumbers, the live rock had an energy I had to admire. Even gobies and rock wrasses darted in and out of my light.

We both inspected the cracks between the boulders. An involuntary side-to-side slide disoriented me. Nothing jarring, but my stomach turned over as if I'd just been hit with mild seasickness. I watched a small stone float between us. Another aftershock?

I glanced at Russ. Feet upward and face up close to a crack, he looked like a strung-up marlin on display. Another rock dislodged and floated to the seafloor. The futility of our search hit me. Even if we were in the right location, what were the chances we'd ever find Jonathan's hideaway after a hundred years of earthquakes and natural water changes?

I glanced at my dive computer and motioned Russ upward. Returning to the surface with five hundred pounds of air just made sense. Forty-five minutes had gone fast.

We surfaced after a three-minute safety stop about fifty yards from where we'd started. In addition to the Doodler, we needed to locate Peter's past search grids. Finding Jonathan's cave by chance was a long shot.

As if it were a ritual, G-paw swam out to meet us. He relieved me of my dive light and led us back to shore, towing the light. My opinion of Peter Gallardo changed then. A dog didn't naturally do what G-paw did. Peter had trained him. The dog's obedience just needed work.

Then why perpetuate the absent-minded-professor persona? Had Chad bought it? He'd have lost the million-dollar finder's fee if Peter had found the Douglas Diamond first.

CHAPTER 11

G-paw rode shotgun, his nose sniffing the Bark U welcome sign when I instructed my car to call Sandy. With any luck, she could use her social media skills and help me locate Chad Williams.

"How was the early dive this morning?" Her cough did not cover her amusement.

"Fine," I muttered. Better than fine actually. I'd never admit that once I'd finished my first coffee, I'd enjoyed the search. No sense giving up my I-don't-do-mornings front without a fight. "We didn't find the cave."

I expected commiseration, not Sandy's upbeat announcement, "I might be some help there. I found long-and-lat coordinates in Peter's notes."

I grasped the steering wheel tighter. Something didn't feel right. "Part of a grid search?"

"Not exactly. It looks like just an arbitrary data entry. Like he'd transcribed the information from another source."

"Another diary?" Could Peter have Skye's missing diary?

That didn't make sense. Even if he did, why would Skye note longitude and latitude coordinates for a local cave?

"Your guess is as good as mine. I also found something you will be interested in." She paused for effect.

It worked. "Come on, Sandy. You're killing me."

Sandy's tsk drew my smile. "You're so impatient."

Admittedly.

"Remember the description of the secret beach where Jonathan had proposed to Marie that you found in her diary?" Sandy asked.

"How could I forget?" Our first adventure together had been solving Jan Douglas's murder. That description had been the clue Jan had been pursuing when she'd been murdered.

"The Cielo Azul logo has the same image imbedded in it."

As far as bombs go, that one ranked as a one-punch knock-out. It connected Cielo Azul to Barkview in the 1920s. "Peter's relative must have been the deported Mexican pilot." It made perfect sense. He'd flown reconnaissance from Barkview to the offshore motherships for Jonathan's smuggling routes. He'd need the coordinates to return nightly in the fog. Sandy knew that. Then why wasn't she agreeing?

"Or Peter's relative was Jonathan himself." She paused to let it sink in before continuing. "Hear me out. Jonathan disappeared in 1925 after a convenient earthquake. The authorities had enough evidence against him to force him to leave Barkview."

A floodgate of possibilities spilled forth. "If Jonathan had survived, he could've returned after Prohibition ended." It couldn't be.

G-paw, sensing my concern, plopped his head in my lap. The gritty feel of his salty hair between my fingers oddly relaxed me. The dog certainly had a way about him.

Sandy continued, "The list of charges wasn't going away.

Regardless, Jonathan would almost certainly have spent time in federal prison. Even Marie said her free-spirited husband wouldn't survive being caged."

"He wouldn't have left her," I said with less conviction. I'd glimpsed Marie's deep love for Jonathan in her writings, but had it been mutual?

"He didn't have a choice. Jonathan Douglas isn't the first man to disappear and start a new life somewhere else." As if to prove her point, Sandy added, "Marie always swore Jonathan was alive."

"I know she insisted she'd know when he died," I admitted.

"Yes. Her diary said she felt Jonathan's loss in 1962. Peter's great-great-grandfather died on September 6, 1962."

A coincidence? I knew better. Could Sandy be right? A sick feeling stirred deep inside me. Was it because I didn't want to believe the fabulous Douglas love story had been an abandoned woman's fantasy?

"Skye left Barkview a month after Jonathan's disappearance. Somehow in 1929 she flies an expensive and innovative aircraft in the first woman's cross-country race. Celeste Barklay disinherited her. No one knows where her money came from or how she managed to compete in the 1930s during a depression."

My finger snagged mid-stroke in G-paw's hair. He jerked his head and looked at me funny, as if I had answers. "I don't believe it." Even I heard the doubt in my voice.

"Here's a scenario. Skye warned Jonathan the cops were in town. He knows the area and lays low for a few days. When he realizes the heat isn't going away, he and Skye run away together. They have that necklace to sell and whatever Jonathan has stashed." Sandy took a breath. "Look on the bright side. It means Skye didn't kill Jonathan."

"It means she was an adulteress." Not sure what was worse

back in 1925. "What happened to the Mexican pilot?" There had to be another explanation. I really wanted one. My admiration for Skye couldn't be based on a lie.

"Records show that the pilot was seriously injured. It's doubtful he would've survived the deportation. The hospitals in Tijuana were little better than hovels back then."

Had the world really changed that much?

Silence strained between us until Sandy said, "It's just something to think about. None of this will be easy to prove."

"Or disprove," I added. The missing diary would solve it all. If there even was a diary. Would Skye record such scandalous behavior? Would I?

"You know, none of this changes Skye's accomplishments as a pilot," Sandy insisted.

"True, but it does change her character."

"It makes her human," Sandy said.

"The world wants a heroine."

"Is that true, or is that what you want her to be?" Sandy asked.

I really hated psychology. Sure, I'd felt a true kinship to the fearless, ingenious woman I'd read so much about. Maybe because I dreamed of being her. In the end, was Skye's story all just another Hollywood drama? Sandy would bury everything right here and now if I asked her to, but much as I wanted to, I couldn't. The truth mattered too much.

"A lot to think about," Sandy said. "What did you call about?"

"I'm heading to see Chad. Can you find him for me?"

"Sure," Sandy said. I heard keystrokes in the background. "You're in luck. He's teaching a class in the Science Hall until eleven. I'll send you the room number and directions. What's he done?"

Happy to be focused elsewhere, I filled her in on Chad's

83

conversation with Jordan and the level of Digoxin found in Peter's blood. No need to remind her about the prescription in Lani's Jeep.

"You know Digoxin is a derivative of foxglove, right?"

It took a second for that to sink in. "You mean if Peter somehow ingested foxglove, it would have the same effects as an overdose of Digoxin?"

"Yup. It's worth looking into. Growing foxglove is restricted in Barkview to keep dogs safe, but it's a honeybee's best friend, and butterfly gardens almost always have some," Sandy said. "I'll check who might grow it in town."

That just increased the list of suspects with access to just about everyone in Barkview. "Keeping digging. Lani needs to be released. I'll tell Uncle G about the prescription."

"Okay. You're still on borrowed time with your mother. You need to call her."

No way. A thousand knives shredding my confidence wasn't going to help Lani any. "My sister called her last night and assured her she was fine."

"From police headquarters?"

"She told Mom she wrecked her phone and ordered a new one." Which was the truth. Had to give her credit for that partial truth.

"The united front of cowardice," Sandy remarked.

My cheeks had to be beet red. "You don't understand."

"Oh, please. Your mother is a five-foot-four and hundred-and-forty-pound..."

"General." Verbalized, it sounded ridiculous. Okay, I admit it. I'm a wimp.

"She's going to find out sooner or later. Isn't it better to just tell her?"

Probably, but I wasn't that brave.

"I see there's no talking to you. I'll dig into Chad's posts and see what connection I can find to Peter."

"And Peter's elusive great-great-grandfather," I added.

"Already on that one. You do remember that Peter had blue eyes, right?"

How could I forget?

"Jonathan Douglas had blue eyes too," Sandy said.

"Something like twenty percent of the world has blue eyes," I said.

"Not in Mexico."

I disconnected the call. That I still instinctively protected Skye had to mean something.

CHAPTER 12

I parked in the visitor's spot in front of the sandstone Science building. On our last visit, G-paw had led us to Peter's office. Today, I leashed him. Too many students milled along the shaded, grassy walkway and on the stone steps for me to keep track of him if he bolted.

An interesting crowd they were, too. Much as I want to believe time had stood still since my undergraduate days in Los Angeles, my eyes didn't lie. Although longish hair and board shorts remained the uniform of the day, piercings and elaborate body art seemed to be everywhere.

I found myself focusing on the Golden Doodle lest I'd be accused of staring as our footsteps echoed in the hallowed hallway. I followed the signs to the lecture hall and nearly got knocked out when the door flew open before a mass exodus. G-paw and I stepped aside until the crowd thinned before peeking in. Chad stood on the dais, his elbow resting on the podium, surrounded by a pack of bleached blondes dressed in crop tops and why-bother short skirts. Chad's khakis and safari shirt failed the Indiana Jones coolness test. The bush hat atop the podium had prop written all over it.

Those crazy mama-bear instincts kicked in again as I marched down the aisle. Chad must've seen me. His toothy grin flattened while his eyes darted toward the exit. Odd. He'd never run from me before. Whatever he said to the students caused a groupie-giggle and less-than-complimentary once-over as they scooted by me.

"Hey, G-paw," he said, still not meeting my gaze.

The dog sidestepped Chad's pet. Easygoing G-paw avoiding someone? What was it about Chad that caused man's BFF to distrust him? At least the Golden Doodle hadn't flashed his bicuspids, unlike the other dogs I'd introduced to Chad.

Awkwardly, Chad stuffed his hand in his pants pocket. "You're here about Peter, aren't you?"

I crossed my arms. No response required. In fact, silence tended to net the best results with him.

"I hardly knew him. We passed in the hall." Chad's telltale flush indicated far more.

I raised my eyebrows. "I find that hard to believe. There are only four professors in your department."

"It's true," Chad insisted, responding as I'd hoped to my just-enough doubt. "Peter was a biologist. I'm a geologist/treasure hunter."

More like a wannabe. "You're sure Peter wasn't looking for the Douglas treasure?"

"The man spent his time in the lagoon." Chad's half-laugh belied any disbelief. "The only thing you'll find there is a sandy bottom littered with inland debris."

That he'd investigated confirmed he'd perceived Peter as a threat. "Then what was he looking for?"

Chad looked both directions and then leaned in to whisper,

"He said it was a starfish of sorts. Peter showed me a picture of it on his Doodler."

I really needed to find that device. I fished around in my pockets for my pink Post-it pad and a pen. The Post-its were easy enough to find. Chad shook his head and handed over his pen. "What did it look like?" I asked.

"I only saw it once for, like, a minute." Chad chewed his lip. "It kinda reminded me of a crooked Mercedes insignia."

Said the status-hungry treasure hunter. I handed him my Post-it pad and his pen. "Draw it for me. I've never seen a three-legged starfish. Can't picture it." Not that I'm an expert on California marine species anyway.

"This didn't look much like one either." Chad drew a few lines. None of which looked anything like a Mercedes insignia.

Skye's charm suddenly felt warm against my chest. I scrutinized the drawing again. Did it have a crude likeness to the charm? I didn't dare compare them side by side in Chad's company.

"Have you seen anything like it in the Barkview caves?" I asked.

"Never. Nothing like it published either. Identifying a new species would be..."

"Career defining," I interjected.

The ticker-tape-parade gleam in Chad's eyes made me wonder just how far he would go for his fifteen minutes.

"Yeah. Tenure didn't matter to Peter. Must be nice to pursue anything you want. You can do that when your family's rich. Did you know his grandfather owns Cielo Azul Distilleries? Can you believe Peter didn't drink either?" Chad shook his head. "What a waste."

Envy, pure and simple, ate at Chad. While he'd blogged, published, and entertained to raise the funds he needed to hunt treasure, Peter's family's wealth backed his pursuits. "Then why did Peter do all that diving?" I asked.

"He claimed he'd linked that starfish to a land-based toxin that might have something to do with the SSWS."

My response disappointed him. "I know about the sea star wasting syndrome. Did Peter think the toxin originated in Barkview?" I couldn't think of a single Barkview business capable of that kind of waste.

Chad shrugged. "Peter didn't say if it was a Barkview company or one farther inland from the dam runoff."

That opened a whole new area of motive. Was Peter's story just an elaborate cover, or could his death have nothing to do with Skye and the Douglas Diamond? My gut told me there was more. "You didn't believe him?" I asked.

"Call me paranoid..."

No argument from me. "You are."

He had the good sense to blush. "Peter asked too many questions about Barkview and the diamond. And the diaries he read were..."

"How do you know about the diaries?" Scrutinizing Peter's reading material didn't exactly fit Chad's style.

"One of my interns helps out at the Barkview Library."

"Why would Peter want the diamond? He didn't need the money," I asked.

"I don't know. It all seemed kinda personal. Seriously, ask your sister. She practically lived with him," Chad added.

I stilled my overprotective heart. Best I keep up the pressure. "Spying on him?"

Chad's flush reddened. "Hardly. Peter lived next door. His front door let out a high-pitched squeal every time he opened it. Before you ask, I tried WD40. Like, a hundred times. That door still woke me up every time he opened it."

The campus party animal and a morning person with a shrill-sounding door between them had problem written all over it. "What time did Peter leave the house yesterday?"

"7:05 a.m."

No need to ask if he was sure about the time. Chad continued, "I do not do well on four hours of sleep. Peter ordered G-paw to stay. That dog paced back and forth on the porch, whining, for an hour."

The Golden Doodle's head cocked to the left. He knew when he was the topic of conversation.

"Then what?" Better to keep Chad talking.

"I taught a class from 10 a.m. until noon. Fifty students will tell you I never left the building."

Likely a valid alibi. "Jordan tells me you've been scuba diving at the Barkview Cliffs. I thought the caves were above sea level," I said.

"Before the 1925 Santa Barbara earthquake. Professor Thomas's source at NOAA discovered a 1939 C-Cap Land..." He bit his tongue.

"...Cover Atlas. It shows the Barkview caves before the World War II blastings closed them off." Anticipation tingled through me. Sandy had been hunting for that report for months. Comparing that map with the 1920s version could reveal which tunnels the 1925 earthquake had destroyed. "Who were you diving with?"

"Some students."

"You mean treasure-hunters-in-training?" Could he be that naive? "With a million-dollar reward on the line, loyalty will come at a high price."

"I..." His open-mouthed surprise seemed laughable. "I'll send you their names."

"Finding treasure is a nasty business." I hated to even go there, but... "Any new insight from your spirit?" That a supposed man of science had consulted with a psychic to find the Douglas Diamond still seemed crazy. Especially when said psychic had her own diamond agenda.

Chad shook his head. "I still have seven months to find it."

My pulse jumped. Deadlines motivated me. "If the prophecy is right and if we're talking about a calendar year versus a lunar year."

Chad slumped, his rear end unceremoniously hitting the floor. "I must find it."

His lip-licking determination stunned me. Something had drastically changed. While Chad had always been ego driven and tended to run from any real danger, desperation had never played a part.

Suddenly, Chad and I both grabbed for the podium as a tremor rattled through the room, knocking his tablet off the podium. Not a biggie compared to this morning, but enough to still spike my blood pressure. "These quakes are making diving hazardous," Chad announced.

No kidding. Russ and I had called it a day after falling underwater debris interfered with our last dive. No sense tempting injury. Fortunately, we hadn't found any promising caves. That would've really tested our safety commitment.

"I have no choice but to continue, whatever the consequences," Chad declared with more bravado than sense, reinforcing my feeling that more was at play than fame and a hefty payday.

On that note, I headed back to my car, puzzling over my strange conversation with Chad. In the years that I'd known him, he'd played the Hollywood treasure hunter part with gusto. Risk taking had never entered the show until now, nor had blatant spying. The man knew far too much about Peter, and my sister, too.

Living next door to Peter offered Chad opportunity. That he

considered Peter a rival also bothered me, considering this new level of nervousness, but that was a long way from motive.

CHAPTER 13

A quick visit with Chad's psychic, Madame Orr, seemed in order. The curtain above the wildflowers and variegated coleus swished as I parked in front of the yellow-and-white-gabled Victorian. No need to call ahead for an appointment. Madame Orr knew I'd arrived.

My last visit here had changed many of my predispositions regarding fortune-tellers, but still I did not trust Madame Orr. Her family's claim to the Douglas Diamond certainly gave her ample reason to find the stone, but we had forged a relationship of sorts.

G-paw paused at the stone walkway, sniffing. Not with concern or trepidation, just interest. As we entered the bright yellow door, a rich agarwood scent surrounded us. As on my first visit, a round, café-sized wood table separating two comfy wing-back chairs upholstered in neutral beige sat in the center of the chic parlor. A deck of oversize celestial tarot cards glared at me from the tabletop. Not another card reading preset to show the dog card?

Madame Orr specialized in putting people off their game.

Not letting her remained the challenge. Sensing my anxiety, G-paw brushed his soft hair against my leg. I rested my hand on his head, oddly calmed. How did this dog drop my blood pressure so effectively?

Madame Orr and her Bedlington Terrier, Danior (more sheep than dog, with its Filbert-shaped ears and pear-shaped head, if you ask me), met us inside. Dressed in her usual shimmering, flowing robe, the large-boned woman seemed to float across the area rug. "I see you've made a new friend, Catalina."

Old news on the Barkview gossip superhighway. I inclined my head, avoiding her heavily charcoaled, dark-as-night eyes. The contrast of her plaited black hair with her pale skin still unsettled me. G-paw contemplated Danior with a mix of curiosity and caution.

Madame Orr tossed her dog a plush toy, effectively breaking that contact. As usual, the sheeplike dog attacked the toy with intent to maim. One squeak later, the dog held the toy beneath both paws while his teeth tore at the stitching.

I swear the Golden Doodle did a double take. No question, Madame Orr's dog was as original as she was.

"Like the rest of us, you will accept your match eventually." The glint in Madame Orr's eyes challenged me to disagree.

Was she talking about dogs or men? I'm sure I flushed.

"I'm here about..."

"I do not know who is discrediting Skye Barklay."

"I didn't expect you would," I replied cautiously. She knew something. Truthfully, I wasn't entirely sure if Madame Orr was a gifted psychic or a charlatan. What I did know was that her intuition rivaled my own.

"I do know the answers will be found in the past. Buried behind a lie," she announced.

I bit back a groan. Her ambiguity made me crazy. Jonathan

running away with Skye would certainly qualify as a big lie. "That's helpful."

"Sorry. What I see is not always crystal clear."

More like never clear and always cloaked in innuendo. "I'm here about..."

"Peter," she finished for me. "He never came to see me."

That made sense. Chad being the exception, most men of science shunned mystics. "When has that ever stopped you?" I suddenly felt like the mouse in the cat-and-mouse game we seemed to be engaged in. It struck me that maybe I didn't want to know this secret. Ugh! Of course I had to know. I always needed to know, regardless of the personal costs. "Surely, someone else..."

"Indeed. Your sister..."

"My sister!" My head was going to explode. Did I know anything about the kid I'd been charged to protect? I suddenly empathized with my-child-would-never-do-that parents.

G-paw butted my arm with his head, snapping me out of my self-recriminations. In retrospect, I should've at least suspected. Mom regularly attended séances. Of course she'd indoctrinated Lani.

I steadied my breath. More ready to listen now, I asked, "What did my half-sister want to know?"

"About Peter's connection to Barkview."

So she'd felt it too. I'd wondered if she had the same intuition I did. "And..."

Madame Orr crossed her arms. "Client privacy..."

We'd been here before. Madame Orr's frown indicated she recalled it and the outcome too. I pushed my advantage. "I can't ask her, Anna. She's in jail. Suspected of a murder we both know she didn't commit."

"You just live to dig up secrets, don't you?"

No argument. I did. In this case it was far more than that. It was personal.

"Oh, all right. She's family anyway. I sensed Peter Gallardo's connection to Barkview. I saw birds."

Skye's charm seemed warm against my skin. "Birds? What kind of birds?" Weeding through her convoluted hints always took far too much energy.

"I don't know exactly."

But she had an idea. I could tell. "Did it look like a vintage airplane? A biplane, maybe?"

She shook her head. "It looked more like a symbol of a bird."

My pulse jumped. Skye's charm did resemble a bird, sort of. That three-legged supposed starfish Chad had drawn suddenly seemed like something else entirely. I searched through my scrunched Post-its pile for Chad's drawing. I laid the sketch on the table. "Like this?"

Her dark eyes glittered in recognition. "Y-yes. It reminds me of an ancient phoenix." Madame Orr's lips curled in a consider-the-possibilities kind of smile. "No denying the symbolism."

"A sign, perhaps?" Her brother, Victor Roma, had named his successful company Firebird Industries, symbolizing the fall and hopefully the subsequent rise of the family fortunes. Not to mention the role of the phoenix in Russian folklore.

"Yes. The color is unique. I saw it in a reddish-golden haze," Madame Orr whispered.

My turn to gasp. Of course, I recognized that description. Anyone living on the beach would.

Madame Orr faced me. "You are familiar with this." It wasn't really a question. She knew I knew something.

"It's the color of sunset over the Pacific during a Santa Ana wind." I let it sink in and then added the zinger. "This is the same symbol Jan Douglas died tracking."

Realization struck. Stuffing sticking out of his mouth, even Danior paused his toy dissection. "We're getting closer," Madame Orr said.

"Closer? Jan Douglas had the image two years ago."

The psychic closed her eyes and massaged the bridge of her nose. I felt her frustration. "The Russian political establishment is poised for change. The timing is critical."

"Victor must be anxious." An understatement, no doubt. He had to be chomping at the proverbial bit.

"Patience is not his strength," Madame Orr admitted. "I'm afraid he will raise the reward for finding the diamond."

That was bad news. Even more treasure hunters would descend on Barkview. "That's all we need."

"That's exactly what I told him. There are already too many competitors as is."

Of which I wasn't a serious one.

"I've told him that the diamond isn't ready to reveal itself yet," Madame Orr stated.

As if the diamond controlled the process. Before I could comment, a small tremor rattled the tea tray. Madame Orr's hand shook as she steadied the china cups. "Unnerving, but necessary."

"Necessary?" My pulse jumped. Madame Orr had just shared something crucial. I knew it.

I'd always suspected there was more to the prophecy than the could-mean-anything words she had shared. "The bear will fall to peasant rule and rise again in the one-hundred-and-twentieth year, when the golden suns unite to revive what was once stolen from the soul of the true leader." I squelched my excitement. "What part does an earthquake play?"

"An earthquake buried the diamond; only another will reveal it."

"There have been many earthquakes since 1925," I said cautiously.

"True, but..." Madame Orr's singsong voice drew me in. I waited for the zinger. "On the eve of the east wind, the golden sun will rise from the shifting sands." She let her words sink in before adding, "We are getting closer."

"Why didn't you tell me this part of the prophecy before?" I asked.

"It wasn't time."

Don't ask me why, but I believed her. The pieces were starting to fall into a pattern. The east wind had to be a Santa Ana wind. The golden sun represented the Douglas Diamond, and the shifting sands had to be the Barkview sandstone rocks moving in an earthquake. All I had to do was locate the symbol, assuming it wasn't fifty feet under water.

One thing I knew for sure: Peter's great-great-grandfather had been part of Jonathan Douglas's smuggling gang. Question was, who was he exactly?

CHAPTER 14

Much as I wanted to run away from my KDOG responsibilities, too many people relied on me. Besides, something told me scanning Skye's diary into the computer needed to be done sooner rather than later. Depending on why Peter had been murdered, whoever had searched Peter's place could well be after this too.

I parked beside Sandy's Jeep in my reserved spot. The original home of the *Bark View*, Barkview's award-winning newspaper, the two-story Victorian's rich reporting history included Pulitzer Prizes and awards from the Society of Professional Journalists, displayed in the historic lobby. Some days I felt my predecessors' frustration as today's fake news challenged their passion for reporting honest, unbiased events.

As I opened the passenger door, G-paw's look questioned my sanity. No argument from me. I lived every newshound's dream, shaping content and information on a popular cable network. Why wasn't I in heaven?

The producing and reporting part I loved and even had talent for. Administration, not so much. Any job that required me to trade proactive decision-making for reactive made me crazy. That Aunt Char had managed the Barklay estate prior to her mayoral election amazed me. I had a lot to learn.

Not that I wasn't capable. I just preferred ferreting out information versus determining if the presented facts added up. And don't get me started on emails. Just keeping my inbox current required constant diligence.

I gave G-paw a minute to sniff and do his business before entering the building. Fortunately, the ritual stick find fit through the door this time. Was the Golden Doodle learning? I doubted it. I'd take the win, though.

I swiped my badge and entered the steel door labeled Employee Entrance. We walked by the lobby and rode the elevator to the second floor.

Although I'd leashed G-paw, he heeled like a trained pro, pressing his warm side against my navy slacks as he walked with the stick in his mouth, his nose skyward, sniffing a frenzy. Curiosity turned to excitement, then anger, and finally concern. I swear the dog experienced the full gamut of my personal emotions in this building. Did he smell that evil Pit Bull my aunt's champion Cavalier had saved me from? Or Gem, Ariana's German Shepherd guard dog, who'd herded me into safe corners? Or Sandy's hyperactive Jack Russell Terrier, who ran circles around us all?

G-paw jerked the leash out of my hand the moment the elevator doors opened and sprinted out, skidding like an out-of-control hockey puck across the polished wood floor. The dog's flaying front paws did nothing to slow his pace, in actuality perpetuating the forward momentum, making me laugh until his shoulder *thunked* into the doorframe.

The noise brought Sandy running into the hall. Dressed in dark slacks and a light-blue button-down Oxford shirt, she looked so much older and more established than the Bark U students. She'd certainly come a long way in the two years since graduation.

Sandy scratched the Golden Doodle's head, then brushed salt crystals off her pants with the back of her hand. "You didn't rinse him off?"

I shrugged. "The dog walks himself and feeds himself. Doesn't he wash himself too? Cats do." Come to think of it, the dog was kind of catlike. My flippancy failed. I got the evil eye from both of them.

"Pacing outside your shower door should've been a clue," Sandy announced.

"Really?" Dual admonishment hurt. "Relax. I have a plan. G-paw will love a visit to the Fluff and Buff Salon."

Realization hit. Sandy's smile widened. "You needed an excuse to check out the speakeasy. I'll send an SOS to Michelle. She'll get you in." Not sure if Sandy's comment was for my benefit or the dog's.

"She always does." Bypassing the normal three-week wait time for an appointment likely had more to do with the Fluff and Buff's owner's soft heart pitying the dogs in my care than my large tip.

I turned over Skye's diary for scanning the moment Sandy confirmed the grooming appointment. A ninety-minute time limit for paperwork was a win for me. I dove into the paper tower with gusto. Hard to believe it had barely been twenty-four hours since I'd been here. A week's absence—let's say for a honeymoon—scared me.

I sorted and prioritized until Sandy's shriek sent me flying across the hall. Hands on her hips, she waved the dreaded forefinger at G-paw.

"What did he do?" Not sure if I needed to protect G-paw or admonish him myself, I stood there with my arms at my side.

"He ate my lunch." She pointed to her desk.

A single bite out of a greasy meatball sandwich could hardly be defined as such. How she managed to stay so trim eating that stuff really was the bigger question. "Clearly, he's smarter than you are. I keep telling you to eat healthier." My smile sneaked through. I couldn't help myself.

Sandy blinked. "T-that's your answer? Your dog is out of control."

"You left it on your desk. Unsupervised is fair game." Listen to me justifying bad behavior. Who'd have guessed?

"It's my desk."

"And how does he know it's your territory?" My logic impressed even me.

Did Sandy's gape portend amusement or an explosion? "He'd better learn. I protect my food."

A drawn dagger came to mind. This wasn't going to end well. Or was it? The telltale gleam in Sandy's sapphire eyes undermined her annoyance. Relieved, I chuckled too. I couldn't help myself. Was I becoming a dog person, tolerant of all sorts of bad deeds justified in the name of cuteness?

Another shriek and an angry "G-paw, you thief!" from down the hall got our attention. We shared a look and sprinted toward the commotion. How had he snuck away without us realizing it?

The dog had done it again. One bite out of an oatmeal cookie. A sample of last night's leftover pasta. Two peanut butter crackers and a gummy bear. G-paw's culinary rampage made no sense. He couldn't be hungry, or he'd have eaten something instead of nibbling. Was he craving something specific? Did dogs even do that? Chocolate got me through stress. Did he have a thing too?

More concerned about him than angry, I found him stretched out in front of my office window, snoozing in a patch of afternoon sun. I crouched down beside him and wrapped my arms around his neck. "Are you okay, buddy?"

Like anyone in a food coma, he lifted his head and gave me a goofy smile. No remorse. Not a care in the world. Why should he worry? The mob was after me, not him. "Okay, Sandy, now what do I do?"

"Simple. Buy everyone lunch." She turned before I could catch a conspiratorial wink.

"Seriously? That's your answer?"

"No. You need to carry treats. G-paw's a grazer."

She couldn't be serious. "That's a thing?" Me, carry stinky dog treats in my pocket? No way. Where would the Post-its go?

"I'm not kidding. Ask your aunt."

"I will." Aunt Char wouldn't mess with me. Or would she?

One look at the comatose Golden Doodle and I shook my head. Why that dog brought out a previously-unknown maternal protective instinct in me remained a mystery. Was this a good thing or not? At this rate, he would bankrupt me in payback lunches in short order.

Score: G-paw 2, Cat 1.

I'd made a dent in my inbox before it was time to take G-paw for his bath and a tour of the long-closed speakeasy with Gabby Turner, our resident barista who happened to be Doc Turner's great-great-granddaughter, as my guide.

With Skye's diary in hand, Sandy shooed the Golden Doodle to the back seat and climbed into my car. "You can now read this on your tablet." Sandy clicked open my briefcase and slipped the rose-adorned diary in.

I nodded. Not that I would. I preferred paper pages, but the insurance felt good. The information contained inside could be important.

"I'm excited to see the Red Door. Skye makes 1923 seem like a blast."

"A time when relaxing with a glass of wine landed you in jail and betraying your neighbors improved your financial circumstances?" I asked.

Sandy frowned. "Times haven't changed much. Up until last year, smoking pot had the same results."

"Point made." Trust Sandy to make that connection.

I turned left on Oak and went around the roundabout onto Third Street. Two blocks later, I turned and parallel-parked on the street in front of the Fluff and Buff Salon.

The three-story Victorian with twin Rapunzel towers occupied a double lot. Four steps led to a wraparound porch with white gingerbread molding accenting sea-green shakes. Once a prominent doctor's home and office, the property featured the main house and a stable-turned-garage that had remained in the Turner family until the area rezoned to retail storefronts in the early 1960s. Today a high-end grooming salon occupied the main home's lower level.

At the glass entry, Michelle Le Fleur whooshed out and air-kissed me, European-style. Dressed in a black smock with a gold logo over black pants and a cap-sleeve top, with a black beret dipped to the right on her poodle-puff hair, she embodied the famed Rive Gauche arts scene. A five-year resident of Barkview, Michelle's Champs-Élysées flair had elevated the canine coiffure scene to local acclaim.

"*Chat, mon chérie,* Gabby is in the *Sanctuaire* with a hammer. *C'est un* nightmare. She is messing with the harmony." Michelle's left hand quivered as she stroked Fifi, the jet-black Standard French Poodle hugging her left leg.

The Versailles-style gardens, touted as a canine nirvana, were surrounded by a thick seven-foot privacy hedge. Michelle air-dried her pampered pets there on plush blue-and-white-striped cushions facing a babbling water fountain.

Sandy scratched her head. "What for?"

Michelle verbalized my thoughts. "She is looking for a red door." Michelle fanned her face. "I told her. There is no door. *Mon Dieu*. The stress is too much."

For Michelle or the dogs? I didn't ask. The talk of the town when a field mouse visited her salon, Michelle tended to over-dramatize everything. I nudged G-paw forward. The distraction worked. Michelle's melodramatic sigh focused on the dog's haggard coiffure. "To the soak." She about-faced and marched inside.

G-paw's open jaw said it all as Michelle led us through the opulent Louis XV–style salon. Set up with individual mirrored stations exactly like a Beverly Hills hair salon, the elegance pressed my WDI Scale's upper limits. (That's my Wright Dog Insanity Scale, my self-proclaimed one-to-ten rating for dog over-the-topness.) Ornate tables in front of gilded mirrors replaced swivel chairs, and private gold-trimmed sinks took the place of washbasins. When we passed by the archway labeled *Sanctuaire*, Sandy and I abandoned the Golden Doodle and slipped out the door.

"We can't just leave him to Michelle," Sandy whispered.

I ignored his beseeching plea. A dog hardly needed rescuing from an expensive bath.

We glimpsed two sunbathing canines as we passed through the *Sanctuaire* and approached the two-story carriage house, where we found Gabby's anorexic Saluki, Sal, pacing like an expectant father. The Victorian building looked more like a quaint granny flat, with its matching sea-green shakes and white trim, than a one-time horse home. A rolled-up architectural drawing stuck out of the greenery beside black apron strings and two feet pointing skyward like a grounded Halloween witch, shouting for help.

"Hey. Lend a hand, I'm stuck." Gabby's call seemed far too calm for an inverted individual.

Sandy and I sprinted to her aid. We each grabbed an ankle and pulled. The workout shoe I tugged popped off like a bottle cap, sending me sprawling backward into the freshly planted coleuses. Ugh! At least I'd changed into dark pants. I still took a limb- by-limb inventory. Unhurt except for my pride, I dusted the mess off my pants as Sandy righted Gabby with a gymnast spotter's flair.

Gabby brushed oval-shaped leaves from her dark hair and patted her barista's apron back into place. Although her lanky, angular look brought a strung-out caffeine junkie to mind, Gabby's warm brown eyes and I'm-your-confidant smile made everyone feel at home. Any wonder her coffee bar, the Daily Wag, shaped public opinion one java at a time. Still, out of her environment she seemed less intense, more supportive.

"I dropped everything. I'm honored to help solve Peter's murder. He was one of the good ones." Her elocution sounded so much like eighth-grade drama class, I wondered if I'd made a mistake including her. As I'd learned, some secrets should never be told.

"Did he come in for coffee often?" I asked.

"Every day at 6:22 a.m. He was a total caffeinator. Man lived on Mexican coffees with extra whip. Figures, right?"

Gabby's theory that personality can be determined by coffee preferences baffled me. "Come on, Cat. The man liked his coffee sweet and spicy with extra cream."

"Meaning he was a contradiction." Gabby's grin confirmed Sandy's explanation.

What did my caramel cappuccino say about me? On second thought, I didn't want to know.

"He didn't come in the morning he died," Gabby added. "Chad did. He met with Doc Thomas at nine. They talked for about ten minutes before Chad stomped out."

"Who's Doc Thomas?" I thought I knew every doctor, lawyer, and shop owner in Barkview.

"Peter and Chad's boss," Gabby replied.

"The dean of Bark U's Science Department?" I asked.

Interesting information. Gabby's gossip did sometimes pay off. I pulled Post-its from my pocket. Sandy automatically handed me a pen to make a note to check with Chad. He could easily have stopped by the lagoon before his class the day Peter had died.

"I'm excited to help. I mean, we did good catching Chris's killer," Gabby added.

Although Gabby's version of the story painted her the hero, I didn't care. Chris's murderer had been arrested.

"Gramma told fantastic stories about the Red Door," Gabby insisted.

"Your grandmother wasn't born until 1940-something. How did she know about the place?" So much for a secret illicit booze joint in Barkview.

"Oh, she knew. Everyone knew," Gabby insisted.

"How did Doc Turner stay out of jail with a speakeasy on his property?" Sandy asked.

Gabby's knowing smile screamed conspiracy. "The Bureau of Prohibition, which enforced the liquor ban, was part of the Internal Revenue Service."

"Not the FBI?" That made no sense. IRS agents weren't trained law enforcement officers.

"And everyone wondered why corruption ruled, right?" Gabby said.

"Don't forget how unpopular the law was too," Sandy added.

"True. Let's just say my great-great-grandfather had connections." Gabby's index fingers made air quotes around the last word. "Did you know doctors could write legal scripts for medicinal alcohol back then?"

Sandy nodded. Of course she knew.

"My great-great-grandfather stocked the cabinets of every top Barkview official, courtesy of Jonathan Douglas," Gabby said.

"So where was the Red Door?" I asked

"Under the garage in a repurposed old root cellar."

"A subterranean bar in earthquake country?" Sandy gulped. I did too. The recent earthquake activity made the whole concept unnerving.

"The walls were solid rock. I bet it's still here, and the tunnels too."

My pulse jumped, my intuition on alert. "You mean there are more tunnels?"

"Yup. While the speakeasy was common knowledge, the underground passageways remained a Tomlinson secret. You asked how I know. Well, the truth is, my granny was a Tomlinson. She always said that she came from a long line of smugglers."

"Smugglers? What did they smuggle into California before Prohibition?" Sandy asked, intrigued.

"I have no idea." Gabby crossed her heart. "My gramma's story."

Sandy's thumbs raced across her phone screen. "Barkview history calls them fishermen who owned a cannery." Sandy confirmed my memory of one of the five founding Barkview families.

"They did. Every family must eventually go legit. Long before Prohibition, the Tomlinsons used their boats to loot shipwrecks."

"They weren't getting rich off that deal." Seriously, how many disabled or grounded ships could there have been off

Barkview's picturesque coast?

"Prohibition should've made them rich. I guess it probably did, except Jonathan Douglas brokered the deal with the motherships to buy the bootlegged booze first."

A light went on. "Quite the coup." And a major motive for betrayal.

"Needless to say, they were reluctant partners," Gabby agreed. "Jonathan needed their ships. The Tomlinsons needed the supply."

"So, the upstart Douglas managed the unruly thieves." That explained the rivalry.

"Tell me more about the tunnels," Sandy said.

"The tunnels were formed by ancient rivers flowing to the ocean through the rocks. Just like the caves at Barkview Cliffs. Every Tomlinson male was jailed the night of the raid, but the tunnels were never exposed."

Had family loyalty run deep, or had they given up their rival leader in a plea deal?

Gabby rolled open the drawings and pointed to a line that ran from the lagoon to the Hounds Hardware building, the closest building to the water. It linked the beach to town. "My great-aunt Zinnia converted the then-vacant garage into exam rooms in the 1940s, when she took over her father's practice."

Today an art studio resided on the second level. The lower level housed a tourist knickknack depot.

"Your great-aunt was a doctor in 1940s?" Sandy asked.

Sandy caught on right away. Was Zinnia yet another remarkable woman unrecognized in Barkview?

"She graduated at the top of her class from Johns Hopkins. The whole family became medical professionals. My great-great-grandparents had six children. My great- uncle Randal became a surgeon."

"Randal Turner's bust is in the Barkview Hospital's entry," Sandy remarked.

"He built the hospital. My youngest great-uncle died rescuing a wounded soldier in Korea. My great-gramma and two of her sisters served in the Army Nurse Corps during World War II. My cousins live in the Terraces or at the beach now. You know Lionel Anderson, right?"

"He's the pharmacist." Sandy's blush got my attention. Was there something going on there I should know about?

The last names had changed over the years, disguising their heritage, but this Barkview founding family continued to shape this town. "What happened to you?" Curiosity stirred. Gabby's family pride impressed me. I'd never really put all the pieces together.

"I am a practitioner too. My drug of choice doesn't require a prescription and delivers a feel-good pick-me-up."

Her enthusiasm hit too close. Caffeine addiction? I cleared my throat. "So how do we get into the speakeasy?"

Gabby checked the map and then beckoned Sandy and me with her forefinger. She switched on her phone's flashlight app and poked her head behind a flowering red bottlebrush. I saw it then, blended almost perfectly into the shakes, a faint outline of a Dutch door. What else would you call a door that only stood three feet above the ground? On closer inspection, more like the top half of a door. The bottom was buried in the grass. No opening that point of entry.

"The door's not red." Sandy's announcement reiterated Skye's observation a hundred-plus years later.

Nor was it recognizable. Seriously, you had to know it was there. Gabby tapped the shake wall beside the half door with the hammer. Bits of shakes crumbled to the ground. She continued tapping farther away from the door. What was she looking for? I glanced at my Google tracker watch. At this rate,

G-paw's grooming would be long over before we found whatever Gabby sought.

"Uh, Gabby..." I said.

"Patience." She wiped a dust streak across her forehead with the back of her hand and continued to tap with more vigor. "It's here somewhere." The hammer struck metal. "Aha! I told you." Excitement bubbled from her. Gabby even posed for the picture Sandy took as she removed shakes, uncovering what looked like a midcentury fire safe.

Gabby referred to the now-crumpled map and typed in a code. The lid opened, revealing a knob. Something clicked when she turned it, and a door swung open in what appeared to be a solid shake wall. My heart pounded as I peered down an abyss of a staircase.

Phone lights illuminating our way, Sandy and I followed Gabby into the inky darkness. Oddly, Gabby's dog refused to follow us, instead planting his skinny butt at the entry. Even I had to duck my head as we entered, making this entrance a hazard for anyone over six feet tall. Were all the tunnels about this size?

Gabby flicked gauzy spider webs aside as a musty, Grandma's-attic odor filled my senses. I sneezed as Sandy read Skye's diary description.

I can't see how the Red Door could ever have been a root cellar. The hip dance club has a stage painted with peacock blue and red geometric shapes. Even the liquor bottles behind the bar shimmer like a rainbow. A black woman dressed in a sparkling sequin gown—my mother would faint if she saw—sang a jazz tune while dancers Charlestoned. Mother demands I learn cotillion for my debutant ball now that we are out of mourning for Father. Never. This is a new time. A new era.

That Skye did know Jonathan Douglas meant nothing. Everyone knew everyone in Barkview. I took a deep breath. I sure felt Celeste Barklay's frustration dealing with Skye's rebellious teens.

Trepidation followed me as I walked deeper into the darkness, not at all sure I wanted to discover the secrets long buried down here.

CHAPTER 15

Three steps belowground, an aftershock shimmied around us. Nothing cracked or crumbled. We coughed in the swirling dust, but pure adrenalin drove us on.

"Solid rock cave" better described the converted root cellar, confirming why a hundred years of Southern California earthquakes hadn't felled the structure. Inside, not a hint of Skye's description remained. Decades of dirt and neglect had reduced any Roaring Twenties treasures to heaps. Only an L-shaped outline of the bar remained.

I saw it all, though. In fact, the craziest sense of déjà vu came over me. Had I really been here before or just read about this jumping juice joint in Skye's diary late last night? I envisioned the dance floor rocking with jitterbuggers and evening gowns glittering in the elaborate wall-to-wall mirrors. I even felt a raw, forbidden kind of excitement that intrigued me almost as much as the smell of Crack's bergamot and sandalwood cologne.

Sandy gave me the nod, no doubt recognizing the crazy

witchiness that took hold of me during investigations, and engaged Gabby. "Was that door the only way in or out?"

"No." Gabby trained her light on the drawings. "My gramma told me about a dumbwaiter that delivered the booze from the ground level."

"It's behind the bar." I gestured toward the boarded-up east wall. Don't ask me how I knew, I just did. I knew a lot of things about this place Skye never recorded, including how she fluffed her hair in front of a fancy peacock mirror on the north wall and how she filled in as the bartender on smuggling nights.

That would have put her in the speakeasy during the fateful raid. Had she been arrested along with half of Barkview's residents that night? History hadn't recorded that fact. Had Celeste covered it up? A Barklay behind bars would never be tolerated. Nor would having only one way out of an illegal operation. There had to be another escape route.

Sandy referred to her phone, no doubt referencing Skye's diary, while Gabby tapped on wooden boards. Their collective "Aha!" drew my attention. "We found the lift," Sandy announced.

"Exactly where you said it would be." Gabby eyed me curiously.

Unless I aspired to be Barkview's newest psychic, I'd better explain away my prediction. "It should be. I read Skye's diary last night," I explained. "She spent a lot of time here from 1922 to 1925. She described this place in detail."

Gabby didn't want to believe me. Not that I blamed her. Buying my explanation meant losing a great gossip trail. I crossed my arms, unbending. Finally she said, "That's really all it is?"

"Sorry. Nothing too cool," I replied.

"If you two are done, I've got something." Sandy pried off a rotted floor-to-ceiling board, revealing an old-time rope pulley system that led to a three-foot-by-three-foot cube. I figured four liquor cases fit at a time, making stocking lengthy. Not that it mattered if the contraband arrived in small quantities anyway.

"I'm going up in it," Gabby announced. "I want to know where it leads."

So, did I. Caution prevailed. Sandy tested the rope's strength. "Not a prayer that's holding anyone."

Gabby flashed her light around the area. "I'll go upstairs and see if I can find the loading point. I have an idea where to look." On a mission, she disappeared up the entry staircase.

Sandy and I shared a look. No holes in that plan. Rolling Skye's strange charm between my forefinger and thumb, I strolled to the north wall. Although every decoration had long since been removed, I knew exactly where that peacock mirror had hung. I tapped my knuckles on the stone wall. The hollow echo stopped me cold. Was this rock merely a facade? I tapped every few inches until a solid, unmoving sound replaced the echo. No doubt about it. I'd found another escape route.

Sandy's cell phone light joined mine scoping out the area. A faint hairline break in the stone indicated an opening three feet off the ground. Sandy snapped her pen tip prying while I searched for a lever. Nothing. There had to be a way to move the door aside.

I'm sure we would've figured it out, except Michelle's sharply accented English shouting at G-paw got our immediate attention. I pictured her scowling, hands on her hips. A moment later the dog materialized beside me, leading an insurrection. He didn't just appear but bounded down the staircase, followed by a once-white Standard Poodle, a right-side-fluffed Lhasa Apso, and a Wire Fox Terrier with a cobweb mustache courtesy of his latest sniff. Michelle did not follow.

Instead, she shrieked from above. So much for the *Sanctuaire*'s relaxation therapy.

G-paw puppy-shook to prove how wet he was, spraying me like a garden sprinkler. My laughter just came out. I mean, what else could I do? "You're in trouble, buddy." I scratched his head anyway.

The Golden Doodle ducked, his ears flat. Was it progress that he knew he'd stepped in it? Somehow this little escape was going to be my fault. I just knew it.

Sandy dusted off the Terrier and Poodle. Even I recognized hopeless looking at the lopsided Lhasa.

"Everything's fine down here, Michelle. We'll bring the dogs back in a minute," Sandy called out, and then said to me, "Michelle is a total taphephobic."

"A what?" I asked.

"She's terrified of being buried alive. She won't even go on a subway," Sandy explained.

There had to be a good story there. One I'd pursue at a later date. Right now, G-paw sniffed the passage entrance.

"We'd better get these guys back upstairs," Sandy said.

One eye on G-paw's exploration, I said, "I vote we hide out down here until Michelle gives up."

Sandy's chuckle came out as a snort. "That could be a while."

And worth the wait, I decided until Gabby's voice joined Michelle's. Gabby telling tales better not shared scared me more than returning the Lhasa.

"You go first." I scooped up the dog and followed Sandy up the stairs. Forget sending G-paw back for a rewash. The scruffy look suited him. Eye level with Michelle's agitated foot tap, I swallowed as I cleared the last step.

Michelle's stream of French expletives, which I knew I didn't want translated, conveyed her annoyance. I just stood there and blinked, allowing my eyes to adjust to the peekaboo afternoon sunlight. In the end, I agreed to pay overtime to repair the grooming mishaps.

G-paw was getting expensive.

Michelle took the three dogs inside while Gabby explained how she'd punched through a sheet rock wall. "Imagine the art gallery owner's surprise when I found the dumbwaiter right next to his hunt scene painting," she added with an impish smile.

At least that adventure offered fresh fodder for tomorrow's gossip stop at the Daily Wag. Cool as finding the dumbwaiter was, it didn't get us any closer to finding the Douglas Diamond

I about-faced at the sound of G-paw's excited bark. He'd found something. I just knew it. Although another tremor unsteadied our footsteps, Sandy and I bolted back down the stairs. Gabby plopped down on the grass beside her dog and refused to reenter.

Phone lights on, Sandy and I searched for G-paw. No dog. Just a waist-high hole in the rocks. OMG! Not only had he opened the bolt-hole, he'd gone through it!

The rock walls groaned around us as another quake scattered debris. "G-paw, come." Even I heard fear in my voice. Was just being here unsafe? "G-paw. Come now."

The distant bark didn't help at all. I peered into the darkness. How long was the tunnel? Could the Golden Doodle even turn around to return?

"I'll get him." Sandy's lip quivered at her offer. "I'll fit better."

No doubt, but... "Absolutely not! That dog is my responsibility." I could kill my sister for dragging me into this mess.

At that moment, all G-paw's amusing goofiness faded, replaced by a certainty that every dog needed basic obedience training. Coming on command could save his life and mine.

"Be ready to dig us out when I figure out where this tunnel goes," I said.

My phone light pointed ahead, I crawled into what reminded me of a navy torpedo tube. I fit, barely. There was no way I could turn around without banging my head. This had to be some cosmic joke. Me, risk my safety for a dog?

I sucked in my breath and moved forward. Every foot I crawled, the rock seemed to close around me. My heart thumped. I told myself to get a grip. I wasn't claustrophobic.

Another déjà vu scene swamped me, even stronger than the last. Skye had been in this tunnel too, escaping from something. I felt her anxiety—make that suffocating fear. That couldn't come just from evading arrest. There had to be more.

G-paw's barking, not incessant—more like a come-on-already bark—kept me moving. As if I'd give up. I'd already sacrificed my slacks and silk blouse. Other than a scraped knee, what could—

Suddenly, the tunnel trembled beneath me. I heard a crack this time, followed by a rock-on-rock crash behind me. I looked over my shoulder. Dust clouded around me, making me sneeze. OMG! Was my return blocked? Did it matter? I couldn't turn around anyway.

My heart raced. Being buried alive wasn't an option. Russ's calm voice reminding me to breathe settled my panic. Keep moving, I told myself; he'd be waiting for me at the end.

I crawled for what felt like forever, until I saw G-paw's curly mop in my light's glow ahead. He sat sphinx-style with his paws facing me. Who was I kidding? Of course he could turn around in the tunnel, unlike me and my generous hips.

He greeted me with an exuberant face lick. Ugh! No escaping that bit of canine love, I guess. I scratched his head. He'd reached the end of the line. A metal door blocked our path. I reached around the dog and focused my light, looking for a lever or switch. Not knowing exactly how he had opened the speakeasy side didn't help.

I banged on the door until my knuckles hurt. No sound from beyond. Or maybe the ringing in my ears affected my hearing. The dog ducked his head under my arm. The apology in his big brown eyes worked until my phone light flickered. My heart pounded. Battery power critical. Any minute now I'd be in pitch-black darkness, who knew how many feet underground. I swallowed, terror threatening to choke me. Did the walls suddenly seem closer?

Now would be a great time for another telling Skye déjà vu moment. Her charm on the chain around my neck pressed into my chest. I felt her strength as if she were here with me, urging me to be calm. I would be okay, I realized. Just as Skye had been. I just had to discover how she'd gotten out.

I held my flickering light right up to the rock. There had to be a way... My light flickered and died, plunging the tunnel into complete darkness. OMG! Talk about a black hole. I couldn't see my nose on my face.

I pounded on the rock. "Help! Help!" G-paw barked again and again. Or was it just the echo? Not that it mattered. The sound was like an anchor in the abyss.

I heard a scrape and click. Or had I imagined it? I'd read about the link between mirages and desperation. Suddenly, fresh air whooshed past me seconds before blinding light flooded the underground chamber.

I shaded my eyes as G-paw scrambled out.

"Cat." Russ's voice had never sounded so good. A moment later his strong arms grasped my shoulders and pulled me the final foot out of the cave. He wrapped me in a hug. "Are you all right?"

I melted into his strength. With the dog pressed against my leg, I knew we'd both made it. I nodded, not ready to speak.

Sandy handed me a cold water bottle. "You had us worried."

Me too. I could've been buried alive down there. "Where am I?"

"The Hound Hardware warehouse," Sandy announced, her nose still in the e-reader diary. I wondered what other secrets she'd uncovered.

"H-how did you find me?" I asked.

"We looked at Gabby's map and a map Russ discovered of underground waterways."

Of course he'd figured that out. Deep down, I'd known he would find me.

"Our educated guess paid off," Russ explained. "This tunnel connects to another tunnel that leads to the lagoon."

"An underwater escape route?" Maybe there was some truth to the Tomlinson smuggling story.

"Perhaps. It is likely collapsed, though." He stopped my protest. "It could not have housed an airplane, even a mono-plane with folded-up wings."

"I scanned the diary for the word 'bolt-hole,'" Sandy explained, "and found Skye's entry when Crack showed it to her. She described a warehouse but never called it out by name. Waiting for you here seemed the most logical location."

No argument from me. I snuggled deeper into Russ's embrace. "Do you still think Peter was an environmentalist with an agenda?"

Russ shrugged.

I eyed him. Vagueness from him never boded well. "But..."

"The chief found papers at Peter's house linking an indus-trial property upstream of the dam project to the realty holding company owning the lot on the north side of the lagoon."

I spun in his arms, dislodging G-paw in the process. Was I trying to make this about Skye when something more sinister

120

was afoot? No wonder I lacked suspects. "Have you traced Peter's genealogy yet?"

Russ shook his head. "Peter's great-grandfather served in the US Army during World War II and became a US citizen for service at the end of the war. He settled in Texas in 1946 and started importing tequila from Guadalajara. There is no birth certificate on record."

"He couldn't be Jonathan's son." I exhaled in relief.

"Unless he lied about his age to enlist," Sandy replied. "If he was born in 1926..."

Russ's look indicated I'd lost my mind. Maybe I had. I still refused to believe Peter was Jonathan's heir. "Don't ask."

"Okay." His phone vibrated in his pocket. Russ checked the screen and then turned to me.

He had to go. I saw his hesitation. At that moment, I realized he would stay if I asked. That was enough.

"I'm okay," I said, nodding. "Is Uncle G releasing my sister?"

Russ looked up from texting. "Someone searched Lani's dorm today. The chief thinks she's safer in custody. Until the Doodler is found, I agree." He'd answered every question succinctly.

I gritted my teeth. "At least she's no longer a suspect."

"I didn't say that. The chief found Lani's fingerprints on Peter's Digoxin bottle."

"She picked up his prescriptions. My sister was basically his assistant." Or mother, the way she anticipated his every need. Russ had better not get any ideas. "Can I see her?" My frustration didn't go unnoticed.

"I'll see what I can do." Russ's lips brushed my cheek. "I'll pick you up at 7:30 tomorrow morning to look for the cave."

He was gone before I could press him further. Probably best for both of us. Whatever he was working on was going to take all evening, I realized. His secrets normally drove me crazy. Not so much today. Was I getting used to the secrecy? Or was it that our goals were the same but approached from different angles?

"Your car is parked outside." Sandy handed me my keys and checked her watch. "I'm late for preshow. Are you sure you're okay?"

I nodded. "I need a hot shower, and so does G-paw." Like it or not, he'd get shampooed again tonight too.

Sandy nodded and rushed out. The dog and I followed more slowly. No need for a leash. He heeled perfectly as we walked through the plumbing department. I ignored the stares until I passed the store window and glimpsed my reflection. Yikes. An aged look. The dust made my tawny hair seem white.

I double-stepped to my Jag and rushed home. Much as I wanted to speak with Chad personally, a call would have to work.

Chad answered on the second ring. "Finders Keepers Treasure Hunters."

"Good afternoon, Cat Wright here." I waited for his grumbled greeting before getting right to business. "I understand you met with Doc Thomas before your class the morning Peter died."

Chad's gasp seemed more surprised than concerned. "You really do know everything."

I didn't, but why dispel that fantasy? "Care to tell me why you stomped off?"

"Do I have a choice?" I pictured his frown. He didn't wait for my admonishment. "Dr. Thomas wanted me to be more like Peter."

Not what I expected to hear. Did she want to feed their rivalry? "In what way?"

"Let's just say that she prefers more traditional publication over undignified blogging and podcasting," Chad explained. "Which is ridiculous. Publishing in a low-circulation professional magazine will not move the enrollment needle."

"Are you short of students?"

"Sciences are down right now, but when I find the Douglas Diamond, the media coverage alone will improve enrollment in geology." He continued, "Doc Thomas is out of touch with today's college-bound youth. Creating content that search engines will love will help me leverage social media followers and engagement and bring in more students."

Sandy basically told me the same thing daily. Even I knew my days of Post-its and pens were limited. How could a dean who worked with students daily not see the value? "Did she want you to take down your website?"

"Not yet. She wanted to talk more about it this week. It's a moot point now. With Peter gone, I'm the only contender for the full-time teaching position."

I froze. Had Chad just revealed a motive? But killing Peter for a low-paying job made little sense.

CHAPTER 16

I toweled my hair dry, anticipating a quiet evening on my sofa with a sandwich and Skye's diary. Half a sandwich, I corrected myself, knowing full well G-paw would demand his share. Not that he'd be hungry. I'd already fed and walked him. He just wanted a piece of mine. That I'd figured that out didn't shock me half as much as it should have. This dog reminded me of my spontaneous younger self, before I'd learned self-restraint. Not that Aunt Char or my mother would necessarily agree I'd achieved it.

I poured myself a healthy shiraz du jour. It was past time I enforced obedience with G-paw too. The trick was not to crush the dog's free spirit while enforcing discipline.

I made a turkey and avocado sandwich and plopped into my comfy sofa-lounge. G-paw joined me, paw in my lap, until I tore off his half of the sandwich. Minus the avocado. I wasn't sharing that. He gobbled it in two bites and snuggled beside me. I didn't bother to shoo him to the ground. His warmth pressed against my hip felt good.

I opened the diary.

August 10, 1922
I am in love. Crack said I am a natural pilot. I felt free for
the first time in my life. Free from Mother's demands. Free
from Barklay responsibility. There's a flying school in San
Diego. Crack teaches there when he's not helping Jonathan.
I can get a pilot's license. Mother never need know.

September 20, 1922
They called me Blue Skye. I am the only woman flying. The
men stare at me. Let them. I am a bird soaring in the heav-
ens. Stick and rudders are my arms and legs. I feel Harri-
son's joy in every thermal. No one can stop me.

Reading about Skye's trials and joys as a pilot warmed me.
She had found her calling and her call name, Cielo Azul. How
Celeste remained ignorant shocked me less after my ignorance
of Lani's adventure. I'd seen only what I wanted to in my sister,
not what was right in front of me.

I ran my fingers through G-paw's hair. He sighed and
scooted closer for maximum reach. Had to love this dog. The
odd thing was, the more I read, the more I wondered exactly
what Skye's relationship was with Crack. Was she really in love
with him, or was it all about flying? Her brother, Harrison, had
encouraged her interest in flight. Crack fulfilled her dream to
fly. In fact, her phraseology mirrored previous conversations
with her brother. Confused, I flipped back to entries referring
to Harrison.

My doorbell rang as the grandfather clock struck nine. G-
paw scrambled to his feet and loped to the door, barking, his
tail slapping from side to side. He either knew my caller or
planned to lick an intruder to death.

I checked my phone. I'd installed a Ring doorbell after the
last break-in nearly cost me my life. Aunt Char waved at me. I

auto-unlocked the door and scrambled to my feet. Aunt Char never just stopped by.

"What's wrong?" I asked breathlessly.

"Nothing serious, my dear. I knew you were up and wanted to talk to you about a meeting I had today." With defensive end precision, the Golden Doodle blocked her entry, only moving aside after she petted him. "I missed you too, G-paw."

I still chewed my lip as I followed her into the kitchen. "Brandy?"

Aunt Char slid onto the corner counter stool. Dressed in her usual suit and heels, with not a hair out of place, she looked like she'd stepped out of a St. John ad. "Yes. Thank you."

I repositioned a few bottles before removing the aged French brandy I kept for her rare visits from my cabinet. Aunt Char indicated I pour a generous amount. Definitely not good news coming.

I topped my shiraz in response and sat beside her. "It's my mother, isn't it?"

Aunt Char choked mid-sip. "You haven't told her Lani's being questioned yet?"

I swallowed my denial. Too bad my flushed cheeks gave me away.

"Catalina Wright, what are you thinking?"

Aunt Char's admonishment hurt. I responded without really thinking. "That I can help my sister better by finding Peter's killer than by dealing with my mother's accusations." My words sounded selfish even to my ears.

"She has a right to know. I would want to know, and so would you."

When she phrased it that way, I felt about three feet tall. I really hated it when Aunt Char went all Freudian on me. "Point taken. I will call her in the morning."

"Hawaii is three hours earlier," Aunt Char pointed out.

Making it cocktail hour. No way I'd interrupt that ritual. "Morning is better. She's more reasonable before she entirely wakes up."

Aunt Char exhaled, clearly not in agreement. "You should know, my dear."

We'd just agreed to disagree, I guess.

"That is not why I came tonight," Aunt Char said.

Now what? I took a long swallow of wine, the usual calmness not materializing. Even G-paw sensed my anxiety. He leaned against my leg in support.

"A representative from the land trust company owning the land on the north side of the lagoon came to see me today. They are asking me to support rezoning the area for docks."

"They want to turn the lagoon into a marina?" I asked.

"The presentation included research on a recreational area with jet ski rentals, kayaks, and stand-up paddleboards. The financial benefits to the city are significant. They also want the old cannery designated as a historic landmark."

I took another sip of wine. "They want you to present the plan to the Coastal Commission?"

"The plan has already been presented."

"That means environmental impact studies have been completed," I remarked.

"I would agree. Adam Smythe claims to know nothing about this either."

That the former mayor pleaded ignorance hardly surprised me. Denial was his best defense since his bid for a congressional seat precluded involvement in any controversy.

"So what's the problem?" My intuition kicked in.

"The state historical designation for the cannery has been stalled," Aunt Char explained.

"And they want you to declare the site a Barkview historic

landmark?" Local designation processes tended to be less onerous.

"It's a deal breaker if I do not."

There had to be more. "What else did they sweeten the pot with?"

"Nothing worthy of repetition," Aunt Char sniffed.

Talk about not knowing their audience. That bribe had crashed and burned.

"I have asked Jennifer to look into the cannery. If it qualifies as a Barkview historic site, I will see that it is properly handled. I found the entire conversation distasteful and suspect."

Her meaning hit me. No way another project rooted in 1920s Barkview could be a coincidence. "We need to find out who the stakeholders in the trust are."

"Agreed. Please give Russ my best." She rose. "By the way, have you two discussed where you will live after the wedding?"

"Uh, no." I couldn't think about it.

"The tenants in 335 Rock Road have given their notice. It might be a nice place for you two to grow into."

Nothing subtle about that suggestion. I wanted to be mad, but why? I loved the sprawling Mediterranean villa. Built by a Barklay ancestor in the late 1940s, the home's endless verandas offered magnificent ocean views. The five-bedroom home also gave us plenty of living space. "That is a bit more than we need."

"Perhaps. The important thing is to have a place you can both call your own."

Aunt Char had a point. My two-bedroom-plus-a-den townhouse worked well for a single professional. Likely not so much for two professionals needing home offices and accustomed to breathing room.

The telltale shine in her eyes indicated Aunt Char had more

to say. "JB and I lived there for a year before his mother passed and we moved to the Barklay Estate. It was a very good time for us." She patted my arm. "I don't mean to interfere. Mention it to Russ." She turned to leave. "Don't let anyone pressure you into choosing a wedding date. This is your celebration, my dear. No one else's."

She didn't wait for my reply. Instead, she downed the last sip of her drink and departed.

Her meaning struck me. Whether I eloped or staged a grand ceremony didn't matter. My happiness did. I felt the pressure melt away. Russ and I had a home now—a place graced with Aunt Char's happiest memories. It portended something good.

If only the rest could be as easily resolved. More questions than answers surrounded this case. How did discrediting Skye Barklay connect to Peter Gallardo's murder and the north lagoon property? Was Peter an environmentalist tracking genuine polluters, or just a random treasure hunter looking for a payoff? Why did my normally reliable gut tell me that solving Jonathan Douglas's disappearance was the key? Skye's charm pressed into my chest. The answers were out there; I just needed to find them.

CHAPTER 17

Sandy showed up at my sliding glass door at 7:20 a.m. while I spooned peanut butter into G-paw's kibble bowl. Dressed in Bark U sweatpants and a sweatshirt and carrying the faded leather log book I'd found with Skye's diary a couple of days ago, she looked intent on a hunt.

"Where's Jack?" Weather notwithstanding, Sandy ran her Jack Russell Terrier with the Jack Pack down the boardwalk every morning about this time.

"Home." Her emphasis got my attention. Her news had to be huge.

"I know where the plane cave is," she announced.

The peanut butter jar fell from my frozen fingers and clanked on the counter. Had Sandy just found the location of the long-lost Douglas Diamond? "How?"

Not to be denied, G-paw's front paws immediately balanced on the counter while his nose pursued the jar, pushing it into the sink. The dog's groan tugged at my funny bone. Forget the sit-and-stay training I'd planned for this morning. We could start his discipline later. I didn't even bother to reprimand him. Instead, I just placed his bowl on the floor and ignored the flying kibble as he dug in.

"That flight logbook you found with Skye's diary repeatedly lists two Barkview locations. When I cross-referenced the dates with moonless nights, I figured out where the plane had to be stored," she explained.

"Great work." No need to feign amazement. Sandy's research skills rivaled a Smithsonian librarian's.

"Listen to what Skye wrote." She read from her iPad:

May 12, 1923
Mother suspects something. She's asking too many questions. Did Tory Rose rat on me? She flew with me today. Her ears flapping in the wind, she smiled all the way. Crack gave me a charm. He has the same symbol on his plane. I asked what it meant and he said that it is a phoenix—a beginning. Marie smiled when she saw it. She wouldn't tell me why. She did congratulate me. Tonight I will fly spotter for Jonathan and the Tomlinsons. One light at Sally Tomlinson's means it is safe to unload in the lagoon. Two lights mean I fly to the cliff cave. If dark, I lead the boats there. If I see a light at the bathhouse, I fly by the boats and give the dump cargo signal. Jonathan says no cargo is worth capture. He protects his friends.
I pray it goes well.
Mother without her brandy is not reasonable.

"So that's how Jonathan confirmed his shipments arrived safely." If the beach was not safe, he used an alternative drop point at the cliffs. Two hiding places... Which location had he chosen that fateful night in 1925?

"One of the locations is located on the east side of the lagoon," Sandy announced.

"Near Peter's murder site?" I asked.

"Close enough," Sandy agreed. "That's no coincidence. Peter had inside information."

No argument from me. The information was also time-specific, known only by the bootleggers themselves—confirming I'd been right all along that the answers would be found in the past.

Sandy added. "The other site is..."

"Near the Barkview Cliffs." I finished her sentence. Of course, Skye would have recorded her flights. All professional pilots did.

"Yup." Sandy referred to her iPad. "High tide is at 8:20 a.m. You can search for the lagoon cave on this morning's dive."

Anticipation tingled through me. "Russ will love a more targeted search area." Our chance for success increased exponentially. "I need to walk G-paw. Tell Russ about it when he arrives." I exited onto the boardwalk before Sandy could ask why I was walking a self-sufficient dog like G-paw. I wondered myself.

Although Sandy wasn't a certified diver, I understood her desire to be nearby. We'd been looking for the Douglas Diamond for almost two years. Madame Orr's comment about the timing being right struck a chord. I still couldn't shake the feeling that only a Santa Ana wind would lead us all the way.

I ignored the dog's quizzical look as I leashed and walked him out to the patio. Not that I'm an obedience-training expert, but I figured laying out my expectations had to help. G-paw had been trained; hopefully only a refresher course would be necessary for the dog to understand my rules and curb some of his impulsiveness.

G-paw heeled like a pro, eagerly following my instructions as we quick-stepped it to the grassy park. He quickly did his business and chose his stick before we turned back. The dog even dropped his treasured stick at the sliding glass door on my command. I called it a win.

Score: G-paw 2, Cat 2.

Inside my townhouse I found Russ and Sandy bent over an iPad, their enthusiasm electric.

Russ broke away long enough to kiss me. "Sandy's information could explain why the police divers discovered an abandoned underwater scooter in Peter's diving area," Russ admitted, almost reluctantly.

Two things struck me. First, would he have shared that information without Sandy's discovery? Second, Peter was no diehard environmentalist. He'd come to Barkview looking for answers. Whether that included a priceless diamond necklace remained to be seen. The big question was, how had Peter known about the cave, and why was the excessive stealth necessary?

Skye's charm pressed against my chest. We were getting closer; I felt it. What part did Skye play, and what did she want me to find?

With Boy Scout precision, Russ led us to the beach nearest the coordinates Skye had recorded, which happened to be a good distance from Peter's murder site. He'd done a good job hiding this location. If Skye's recordings were accurate, a hundred years ago we'd have been standing in front of a cave opening concealed by brush. Today, fifty feet of brackish water obscured the entrance. Had the cave withstood the many earthquakes and water weight pressing down on it?

Only one way to find out. I shimmied into the Farmer John wetsuit bottoms and bodysuit thanks to my slippery nylon skin and Sandy's help tugging. Covered from head to toe in neoprene, with only my lips and eyes visible, I started to sweat as I lumbered behind Russ to the rocky water's edge. That my waddle failed the ladylike test didn't frustrate me anywhere near as much as how Russ made hauling forty-something pounds of equipment on his back look easy.

G-paw watched us from the shoreline, leisurely chewing on his stick-du-jour with his front paws in the lapping water. The dog didn't even flinch as we lumbered by him for our beach entry. Waist high in the water, I put one hand on Russ's shoulder for balance as I put on my flippers, took a breath from the regulator, and went right underwater. At the bottom, I switched on my high-powered LED headlamp and waited. Russ's light about blinded me when he arrived a few minutes later. He checked his compass and indicated our direction. I hugged Russ's side as we swam along the rocky bottom, glad for the extra nylon skin beneath my wetsuit. The water seemed colder today. Maybe the aboveground gloom played a part. The lack of sunlight also affected visibility. Twenty feet below the surface, the water distortion made shadows seem ghostly. Now I'd gone nuts. There was nothing supernatural about this quest.

We followed the rock edge until it abruptly dropped thirty feet and Russ signaled our arrival. We split up then, focusing on different sections of the rock wall. Only the calming sound of my breathing and bubbles from each exhalation surrounded me as I searched for an opening. Searching for this cave really felt like looking for the proverbial needle in a haystack. Even having specific coordinates hadn't helped. The structures in this area seemed solid, with only small crevices. I still refused to be discouraged.

The forty-minute dive went too fast. My air gauge read 500 psi as we headed to the surface. About ten feet up, something red fluttered on the bottom. I stopped kicking and squinted, but the vision faded. Had I imagined it? I rechecked my air and decompression time gauge. Four hundred psi wasn't danger-ous. I gestured to Russ. If you wanted to test a relationship, try scuba diving. Here, muffled grunting and hand signals passed as primary communication, making justification all about faith.

Russ checked his air gauge and gestured for me to lead. Together we kicked downward. He must've thought I'd lost my mind when I swam past the latitude-longitude points to a small rock pile in the sand. We circled from opposite directions. Nothing. It was here; I could feel it. But my air gauge read 200 psi, and my dive computer indicated a need for a two-minute decompression safety stop. I shrugged and pointed toward the surface. Russ nodded and we kicked up.

It must've been the water displaced by my fins, but I saw it again, that red ribbon floating above the sand and then settling back down. Without hesitation I dove, clearing my ears as I reached the band moments before a fresh layer of sand covered it. The band was made of rubber, the kind used to float glasses. The only way it could remain underwater was if something anchored it. I followed the line to the sand and uncovered a clear case with a small computer inside. Peter's Doodler? Lani had said it had a red lanyard. Who else would lose a mini-computer in this area? Or had it been hidden? Did Peter suspect something foul at his beach site? He had used an underwater scooter to further disguise his search area. Question was, whom did he suspect?

Russ saw it too. He pointed to the surface. No time to check if the underwater seal had been unbroken. We ascended, stopping at fifteen feet to off-gas. Russ surfaced a few minutes before me. My decom cleared on my dive computer as I sucked my last breath out of the tank, and I exhaled as I shot to the surface. I drew in a few breaths before disengaging my BCD and dog-paddling to shore. When G-paw saw us, he jumped in.

Russ met me waist-deep in the water. I handed him the

Doodler before he could say a word. "I didn't know if I could find it in the sand again on the second dive."

He hugged me close. "You took a risk..."

That he really cared warmed me. Deep down I knew it, but a reminder never hurt. "You'd have done the same thing, and you know it."

He pressed his lips together, officially acknowledging nothing. G-paw swam up and pulled the BC from my grasp. Like a seasoned pro, the dog dragged the inflated BCD, tank, and regulator octopus to the beach, as he no doubt had for Peter dozens of times. Russ squeezed my hand and took my fins in the other. I knew he hated it when I put myself at risk, but this was really nothing. I'd pushed the decompression tables and left my buddy. Granted, not smart recreational diving, but nothing really dangerous.

Sandy's "You rock!" made it all worthwhile. She'd rolled up her sweatpants to knee length and met us in the water. She inspected the pouch as she took the Doodler. "It's dry. And," she said after powering it up, "not password protected. Battery is low..."

Not that a password mattered. Sandy seemed able to crack just about anything. Russ and I shared a glance. No need to say more. Sandy had gone into nerd heaven.

We sat on the sand with the Golden Doodle between us, waiting. A few minutes later, she said, "Lani was right. Peter was a talented artist. I'll download all his pictures later. These were his last drawings."

I shaded my eyes, not from bright sunlight but the May-gray glare. A large rock arch camouflaged by overhanging plants above and bushy scrub and red bougainvillea below filled the screen. A cave fit for Jonathan's romanticism. Sandy's forefinger swished the picture aside. The next image showed a cropping of rocks alive with colorful underwater organisms. No likeness between the two.

"Is that supposed to be the same place?" I verbalized what we'd all been thinking. Where had Peter seen the original aboveground cave? Had he created it from stories or actual pictures? What did the second picture represent? Had Peter located the original cave and determined it had been destroyed in the earthquake?

Russ took the Doodler and studied the drawings side by side. "The width appears to be similar." His doubts affected me more than I cared to admit. "I can run an earthquake simulation program..."

"You can do that?" I asked. Russ's capabilities always impressed me. Who even knew those programs existed?

Russ nodded. "The computer can estimate damage based on the type, duration, location, and magnitude of the quake. It's currently used to create damage estimates. There's no guarantee it will be accurate, though."

"Chad Williams wrote a paper on the technology. He published it in an obscure seismology magazine a few months ago." Sandy didn't look up from the Doodler.

That got my attention. I swear Sandy knew everything, but this was over the top even for her. "How do you know that?"

She tossed her ponytail over her shoulder. "Peter noted it here." She pointed to a scribble on the Doodler.

My intuition twinged. How had Peter learned about the publication? Had he chided Chad about it? Chad's sense of self-importance couldn't begin to cope with any comparison between Peter's potential new species find and an insignificant publication. If a full-time teaching position hung in the balance...

Now I was reaching for a miracle. I took another long look at the rock pile. Did knowing the damage estimates really matter? Locating a specific pile of rocks underwater, even with a picture, was next to impossible.

I glanced at my watch. Time to go in for the second dive. "We have a location, and we know Peter was searching in this area." I leaned over Russ's shoulder to see the rock formation. The cave was there, I knew it. "Let's see if we get lucky."

We found nothing on the second dive. Fortunately, Sandy had picked up additional scuba tanks. "Third time's the charm," she grinned. "And I think the coordinates are off by a few degrees." She laid out complicated reasoning having to do with water displacement and the dam flooding back in 1930s I didn't pretend to understand. "I called Chad Williams about it. He said he and Peter discussed the same possibility last week."

And now Peter was dead, and Chad had motive and opportunity.

Russ read my agitation perfectly. "We need evidence." He handed me my fins.

I knew that.

"Before you go, you need to see this." Handing me the Doodler, Sandy said, "I give you the Douglas Diamond."

I sucked in my breath. Two years of wondering and hoping vanished as I looked at the magnificent fancy yellow oval-shaped diamond flanked by two brilliant teardrops mounted on a diamond strand. It was a necklace fit for a princess. A royal princess.

That Peter had a drawing didn't surprise me. No secret he'd had inside information. He hadn't seen this necklace personally, though. The drawing lacked fire. I'd seen the Shepard Diamond up close. The stone's depth had a life of its own.

The pieces of the mystery still spun around in my head as Russ and I hiked down to the sandy shore. Chad would've lost it if he'd seen the Douglas Diamond on Peter's Doodler. He had motive and opportunity. He knew both Peter and my sister's schedules. All I needed was evidence.

With a direction in mind, we entered the water. Something was different about this dive. I realized it the moment we reached the bottom. The rocks seemed smaller and stacked, creating crevices and openings filled with an abundance of California spiny lobsters. A diver's paradise for sure during hunting season. When a large seabass came out of nowhere, nearly bumping us in its exit to the sea, Russ switched on his LED light and more thoroughly inspected the wall. There had to be a large hiding place. That fish had come from somewhere.

We peered up, under, and around every shelf and outcropping. Russ even flipped upside down to examine the gravel bottom. Nothing. I reviewed our bottom time. At this depth, roughly ten minutes remained. I stroked the neoprene covering Skye's pendant against my chest. We were close—so close. I grabbed Russ's arm and led him to an unusual half-moon-shaped rock jutting out of the wall. Nothing familiar about it, just a feeling.

Russ's grunt drew me to his side. He pointed wildly into the crevice. My gaze followed the light beam. Behind the rock wall, like a ghostly shadow in a haze, I saw it, a narrow, vertical configuration that could easily be a propeller propped up on its side. OMG! Had we found the airplane cave?

Emotion about choked me. This cave was hardly larger than a three-car garage. Even with the wings vertical, no floatplane would fit inside. The boulders piled along the perimeter and scattered around the bottom could indicate a structural collapse.

The size could offer a refuge for smaller boats, but I saw no indication of cargo crates or a hidden boat either. Not that I expected a wood-hulled fishing boat to have survived the elements, but colorful remnants of the liquor bottles should be visible. How cool would it be to find a hundred-year-old brandy bottle?

Russ pried away a few rocks, opening a reasonably-sized pass-through. His attempt to dislodge another key boulder failed. More robust equipment would do it. I assessed the hole. Much as I appreciated Russ's wide shoulders, they wouldn't make it through, but if I sucked in my gut and hand-carried my tank, I could. Would Russ go for it? I knew the risks. Although they'd slacked off, aftershocks had been affecting us all week.

I laid out my plan in cryptic sign language. Russ understood, all right. He crossed his arms and vehemently shook his head. I pressed him. I got his point. We'd get a recovery team here in a few hours. Call me impatient. I had to know now if Jonathan was in there. So much more needed to happen if he wasn't.

I gave Russ the two-minute sign.

I don't know what finally convinced him, but instead of stopping me, he unbuckled my tank, held it steady as I swam through the opening and handed it to me inside the cave that would rewrite Barkview's history. Inside I saw the jagged edge of the ceiling, indicating that it had collapsed. I glided over the ghostly bottom, which looked more like a thriving reef for small fish and a family of vibrant California garibaldis than a 1920's airplane. The sea repurposed far better than the land.

In an effort not to stir up the sandy bottom, I flutter-kicked and floated the rest of the way to the far wall. I shone my dive light across the interior. No colorful glass, no crate wiring or nails either, just a single shining object calling me to it in the swirling sand. I scooped it up and returned to the opening in the allotted two minutes.

I got out just in time. Another small tremor ate away at the opening as I squeezed through. Going in had been the right move. I pressed a pitted metal symbol into Russ's hand as we started our ascent. I'd recognized it the moment I'd picked it up. The same symbol hung around my neck, was embedded in Cielo Azul's company logo, and had been drawn in Marie Douglas's diary to mark the romantic beach where Jonathan had proposed to her. Madame Orr had recognized it as a phoenix, the symbol of new beginnings.

I'd hoped finding Crack's plane and connecting Peter and Cielo Azul to him would prove the man's lineage. It did not. Skye's missing diary and Jonathan Douglas still needed to be found. Fortunately, Skye's coordinates gave us one more place to look.

CHAPTER 18

Coming off the adrenalin high surrounding our find, it took me until noon to run out of excuses to inform my mother about Lani. Deep down, I'd hoped to have solved Peter's murder and avoided the call altogether. Not the case. Finding Crack's airplane only linked Peter to him. It did nothing to exonerate Lani of Peter's murder.

I paced the length of my living room, finally sitting in my most comfortable lounging position while I looked up her number. G-paw, sensing my anxiety, crawled into my lap and licked my chin until I shooed him away. What was it about big dogs thinking they were Chihuahuas anyway?

No more excuses. I had to call my mother. I'd even written down exactly what I planned to say. I still held my breath until voicemail picked up. I left a quick, generic message and hung up. Sheer relief flowed through me. I'd just bought myself another eighteen hours to clear Lani, since the next flight out of Oahu would be a red-eye. Maybe it was my lucky day.

I sure hoped so as I drove toward the Barkview Cliffs. Considering our success finding the cave, Russ had scheduled an afternoon dive to explore the second set of coordinates at low tide. I'm not sure how I felt about this one.

I absently scratched G-paw's head as I drove, until my phone rang and sudden panic rendered me speechless. Then the caller ID announced the Old Barkview Inn. More curious than concerned, I answered.

"Franklin here, Miss Wright." Barkview's premier concierge calling me? I pictured him standing in his Victorian waistcoat and gentleman's ascot and speaking into the fancy old-fashioned dial phone. That Franklin had worked with me to capture Chris's killer put me in his debt.

This couldn't be good news. "What's wrong?"

Any question he took customer service to a level five-star resorts could only aspire to vanished the moment he responded. "Nothing, Miss Wright. Just an oversight."

Why did it feel like so much more than that?

"After reviewing this evening's airport pickups, I came across someone I thought you might be interested in."

"Thank you, Franklin. I appreciate your help," I said cautiously.

"You are welcome. Mary Ann Ohana arrives on Hawaiian Airlines at 8:45 this evening."

I sucked in my breath. So much for escaping from my mother. No wonder she hadn't responded to my earlier message. She was already en route to Barkview. At least I'd called and left a message. I silently thanked Aunt Char for guilting me into it.

How had my mother found out? Aunt Char wouldn't have tattled. It wasn't her style. Lani not being at her beck and call must've done it. Mom might be a lot of things, but she wasn't blind.

"Thank you for reminding me, Franklin. No need to send a car. I'll pick her up."

"I expected as much. Shall I cancel her reservation as well?"

Ugh! My place wasn't big enough for my mom, me, and G-paw. Housing her at the hotel would be easier, for sure. "Yes. Cancel the reservation. Thank you again."

"Family harmony," Franklin said. "Have a nice day."

Not likely. A tornado of emotion dropped down on me. Why couldn't my mother have just called me and forgone the I-caught-you drama? The same reason I hadn't called her about Lani. Sneaking into town to catch me doing something she disapproved of was just like her.

I should have just left her at the airport, but I wouldn't, and she knew it. Much as her games annoyed me, she was still my mother. I had to admire how well she'd manipulated me with this one. Not only was I picking her up at the airport, but she'd be staying with me as well. Ugh! I still had six hours to solve Peter's murder. Talk about pressure.

CHAPTER 19

I met Russ and Sandy on the beach directly in front of Lifeguard Tower One. Built more as a stationary beach-changing room in the 1920s and then elevated to a lifeguard tower during the surf-crazy 1960s, the mint-green-and-white Victorian shack sat on redwood stilts. Nestled closest to the bluffs overlooking the Pacific where Barkview's elite resided, tower number one provided access to the tide pools and coastal cliffs reachable only at low tide. Which was exactly why we were here.

I felt like I'd come full circle. Two years ago in this exact location, Sandy and I had found Jan Douglas's body. She was murdered while searching for the Douglas Diamond with none other than Chad Williams at her side. I had to wonder what role destiny played in life.

G-paw jerked the leash out of my hand and took off across the sand the second he recognized Russ. That the two of them had bonded seemed good until exuberance overtook discipline yet again in the Golden Doodle. Ugh! Just when I thought we had heeling covered. I needed to correct the dog, but breaking up the two boys rough-housing together would make me Disney's Cruella de Vil.

I rolled my eyes at Sandy, who bit her lip trying to contain a smile. G-paw had me trained better than a trick dog.

Score: G-paw 3, Cat 2.

Call Russ a magician. How he managed to locate and deliver a fifteen-foot, hard-bottom, scuba-ready inflatable with a stealthy electric motor to the beach on short notice amazed me. I steepled my hands and yoga-bowed to him. "Oh great one," I teased.

Russ's smile was pure joy as he ordered G-paw to sit. The dog obeyed with an endearing lopsided bark. "Don't thank me. The chief arranged for all this while working on the lagoon salvage with the Coast Guard."

I nearly choked on my relief. I should've seen that one coming. No one had ratted me out to my mother. The good old military grapevine had gotten word to her about Lani. No doubt Coast Guard brass in Hawaii received regular updates on Lani since her father had been a ranking commander. I never had a chance with Lani. Mom had been helicopter-parenting the whole time.

"You okay?" Russ touched my cheek.

I nodded, more determined than ever to prove her wrong. "My mother arrives in six hours. I'd like to get this solved by then."

No questions. Just a joint "Then let's get to it" from Russ and Sandy helped me to focus. G-paw leaped right into the boat and sat at the bow, waiting.

Sandy helped me into my damp wetsuit. Although the sun had temporarily broken through the persistent May fog, I still shivered, but not from cold. We were getting closer. I could feel it.

I glanced at the fogbank hanging like a curtain offshore just beyond Bark Rock. The breeze would be up soon, bringing ocean chop and drizzle and making the ride to the rocks bumpy. I thought about my Hawaii-acclimated mom freezing and made a mental note to bring a sweater to the airport.

"Chad's gone off the social media grid," Sandy said. "I'll bet he's out here diving. His last post was at the Old Barkview Inn's boat dock."

"Who was with him?" I asked.

"A couple of undergrads posted they were treasure hunting today, but there was no direct link to Chad. I'm heading to the Barkview library to help Jennifer research where the Tomlinsons disappeared to after the raid." Sandy turned to Russ. "Any luck on finding who the principals are in the Land Trust?"

Russ shook his head. "Ownership is sealed."

"Seriously? That's legal?" I asked.

"Afraid so. It's the same loophole Disney used to expand in Orlando," Russ explained.

"Can't we use the 'It's evidence in a murder investigation' card?" I asked.

"If we had evidence," Sandy pointed out.

I hated logic sometimes. I lumbered into the inflatable boat, feeling about as nimble as the Pillsbury Doughboy. Russ pushed the boat out past the surf, climbed in, and ended up at the tiller, a testament to his agility. I perched on the opposite pontoon, smelling fresh air and sea salt. Although we hugged the shore, the ocean waves still lapped against us, causing sea spray to drench us and double-down on my already-bad hair day.

G-paw sat in the bow, taking the water head-on like an old-time figurehead as the little boat lurched forward. I'd like to say he looked majestic, but with his eyes closed and tongue hanging out, he looked like a goofball. Exactly what I needed to clear my head so I could save Lani.

It struck me then that G-paw's de-stressing technique worked for me. I got exactly why serious Peter had bonded with this dog and why I, normally a fanatical disciplinarian, let him get away with ridiculously bad behavior. This dog was all about fun—something I clearly needed more of in my life.

Somehow Russ sensed my thoughts and rested his hand on mine. I had a great helpmate to support me. As much as I enjoyed G-paw, I didn't really need him, but Lani did. She'd liked Peter. Losing him had to be devastating for her. I had to prove her innocence.

On that note, I focused ahead. Twenty yards off the rocky shore, a smaller inflatable boat flying a diver-in-the-water flag bobbed exactly where Russ's compass pointed. We'd found Chad's dive site—the same site Peter had noted in his Doodler.

Russ slowed the engine as we approached the boat and drifted into the shadow beside it. A single capped scuba tank aboard indicated a lone diver. Did anyone dive with a buddy anymore? I guess when you're looking for a treasure, more is not merrier. Too bad guilt by GPS location wasn't prosecutable. Although Chad had admitted to spying on Peter, with only circumstantial evidence we'd need a confession to prove murder.

Russ knew it too. "The visibility isn't bad today. The diver will see us at twenty feet," he said. "Drop me off here. Go two hundred yards to the south and wait for my signal."

Leave him in the middle of the ocean on a small boat to wait for a potential killer? No way.

"Cat, this is what I do."

His matter-of-fact tone made me grit my teeth. I guess deep down, I'd never really thought about just how dangerous his job was.

"Relax. I do this every day."

Not helping. His utter calmness didn't surprise me. The

feeling that I did not want to meet him in a dark alley did. No wonder I always felt safe with him.

"Go. We don't have a lot of time," he ordered.

I could argue or trust him. I swallowed my fear. With G-paw pacing on our boat, rocking it from side to side, remaining undetected seemed impossible. I held our boat steady as Russ climbed into Chad's boat.

I motored away and dropped anchor to wait. One eye on Russ and binoculars in hand, I scanned the rocky shore, searching for the symbol woven throughout this investigation. The image that graced the beginning of so many events: Jonathan and Marie's life together, Skye's flying career, and perhaps for the Roma family—if the Douglas Diamond really was found—their destiny. It had to be here somewhere.

The lumpy ocean swell didn't help, nor did the peekaboo afternoon lighting. The prophecy had predicted the east wind would direct us. On a west-facing beach, what would an orange western sky illuminate? I considered a few protruding rocks, but nothing looked promising. Since the Santa Ana winds generally arrived in October, I had four months to narrow down the search area.

I continued my visual search until the unsuspecting diver surfaced. I watched in awe as Russ hauled the man aboard. G-paw watched too. Like a boxer, he swayed and bobbed, finally leaping into the water. He swam with propeller-to-the-butt speed to Russ, barking all the way. Stunned, it took me a second to quickly steer the inflatable in Russ's direction. I could get Chad to talk. I knew I could.

Except the diver wasn't Chad. Jordan Thompson sat cross-legged in the boat with sweat pouring down his face in his wetsuit. "I swear to you. I didn't kill Peter," he kept repeating. "Peter left his Doodler in the wagon about a week ago. That's how I know about this location. There's nothing in the cave."

Jordan jerked his fingers through his damp hair. "Just some blue, dark brown, and lilac glass pieces."

I frowned. No need to say a word, Aunt Char's "let-them-speak" philosophy worked. Jordan added, "No diamond necklace. No boat parts. Nothing."

"Were there bodies inside?" Russ asked.

"No!" Jordan insisted. "The cave collapsed a long time ago. The marine growth is extensive. The recent earthquakes must've loosened the rocks because the opening is new."

My pulse leapt. Madame Orr had predicted the earthquake's importance. Why hadn't he found the necklace? Because it wasn't time yet. Ugh! The psychic's voice in my head was maddening.

I scrutinized Jordan. Would he have killed to find the treasure? My intuition said no.

"I'm surprised you're a treasure hunter. You've lived in Barkview long enough to know the Douglas Diamond is lore," I said.

"The million-dollar finder's fee is incentive," Jordan muttered.

Was this about money after all? "You own a successful business," I said.

"I work eighty hours a week hauling tanks and holding the hands of inexperienced divers who never should've been certified." I recognized a soapbox lecture coming, "I came to Barkview to protect the reefs, not destroy them."

His vehemence sounded real. Russ thought so too. His stance shifted to neutral. "Word around town is that your dog refused to leave," I continued.

Jordan chuckled. "It's a good story. Truth is, I'm more of a betta fish kind of guy."

Knock me over. "No kidding." What else could I say? He'd sold the grieving-dog-owner persona to an entire town.

"You're not alone, Cat. There are others who aren't dog people in this town."

Another secret Barkview society? Now that would be worth researching. I refocused. The ever-so-slight twitch in Jordan's jawline indicated there was more. I needed some leverage, something incriminating to keep him talking.

Suddenly, I had it. He'd had opportunity. "The planter in front of your shop is a butterfly garden, right?"

Jordan's confusion seemed real enough. "Yes. You wrote the article on the area's pollination experiment."

I nodded. Sandy had, actually. "Your garden included foxglove?"

"Yes. It's potted in a raised bed so no dogs are injured by it," Jordan said. "Foxglove is a butterfly favorite. It's... Wait a minute. I thought Peter drowned. Was he poisoned?"

He'd put that together quickly.

"Why did you replant the planter in front of your shop?" Russ asked.

"I told you, some animal must've gotten in it. It was trampled when I arrived on Tuesday morning. I replanted that evening." His story hadn't changed. Why did he seem so defensive?

"That was pretty quick planting for a busy man," Russ remarked.

"My lease requires I have flowers in the bed at all times. The landlord is a stickler."

I shared a glance with Russ. We were on the same page. "I'm willing to bet one of your missing plants was foxglove."

Jordan bit his lip. "I want a lawyer."

"We're not the police officially questioning you," Russ said.

I touched Russ's arm. He got my message and gave me center stage to continue. "We just want the truth, Jordan."

"The plant was outside. Anyone had access to..." Jordan

suddenly went quiet. "You know, Chad admired the butterflies and asked me what flowers I had in the garden last week."

"Chad commenting on butterflies?" Skye's charm seemed warm against my chest.

"Right? I didn't think anything about it until right now."

Chad had access to foxglove. Too convenient?

"Did you ever talk to Chad about his dive locations?" Russ asked.

"He was very secretive. He knew about Peter's coordinates too. I watched him dive here from the beach several times. He abandoned this location last week and moved farther south."

I knew why. Chad had followed his seismologic displacement theory after discussing it with Peter. That the theory seemed valid in the lagoon, but not on the coast seemed odd. I didn't even want to think about why.

"Who did he dive with?" Russ asked.

"Mostly coeds. Rarely the same people."

Jordan's quick answer made me wonder just how many times he'd followed Chad.

"Chad's paranoid and desperate. I feel like he's looking over his shoulder every time I see him," Jordan added.

I'd sensed Chad's anxiety, too, but I'd attributed it to frustration with his boss on our last meeting. Could I have been wrong? Chad had been looking for the Douglas Diamond for a long time. Could he have debts?

With nothing more to ask, Russ sent Jordan on his way. "I still think he has more to tell," I said.

"Maybe. An in-depth background check may answer it," Russ replied. "And a tail."

"You don't think he killed Peter, do you?"

Russ shook his head. "Though he is a quality actor."

I agreed. Disappointment still swamped me. Was Sandy right, after all? Had Jonathan run away with Skye? She had admired him, but she'd loved Marie too. Skye wouldn't do that to a friend.

"It is possible that Jonathan was lost at sea," Russ said.

I exhaled. "Yeah. That makes the Douglas Diamond unrecoverable." Victor Roma, the chairman of Firebird Industries, was not going to want to hear that possibility. Nor would any other Barkview treasure hunter.

"There could also be another cave," Russ suggested.

"And we have no idea where to look." The location of Jonathan's secret beach still eluded us. I needed the missing years in Skye's diary. She had more to tell me. I just knew it.

CHAPTER 20

A quick dive to the smuggler's cave confirmed Jordan's information. As we bounced across the waves back to the beach, I realized we had nowhere else to look for answers or suspects. Except for circumstantial evidence pointing to Chad, we still had nothing. With my mother's imminent arrival looming, my anxiety skyrocketed. I turned to Russ.

"Could Peter's death have been a tragic accident? He was pretty absentminded. It's possible he accidentally overmedicated himself."

"Then why would someone go to the trouble of framing your sister and searching her dorm room?"

I hated it when he pointed out the obvious. At least he believed Lani to be innocent. "Could this be about Lani or...?"

"Or her father, Commander Ohana?" Russ completed the sentence for me. "There are things I can't tell you, Cat."

I took a deep breath. We'd come full circle to his job and the secrets that still ate at me. "I know." I meant it, I realized.

"I promise you. I will not allow your sister to be punished for something she did not do."

I reached across the bouncy boat and squeezed his hand. I believed him. I'd really always believed in him. It was enough.

He smiled and kissed my hand. G-paw wrecked the moment. Like a springboard diver, he took a flying leap off the bow, belly-flopping for maximum effect. Freezing seawater and bits of kelp splashed on me, sending me diving for a damp towel. "That dog..." I screamed.

Russ laughed and kicked up the speed to keep pace with the dog racing us to shore. G-paw won. He bounded up the sand into the oversized towel Sandy held for him. She quickly wrapped him in it and hugged him dry. Her broad grin kicked up my pulse.

"You found the Tomlinsons."

"Yup." Sandy handed me a warm towel. "You first. Did you find the cave?"

I nodded. "It was a bust. Your news is better." I could feel it.

Russ came up behind me to wipe his face on the corner of my towel. "You look about ready to explode, Sandy. Out with it."

"You know the Tomlinsons were arrested when they came ashore at the lagoon during the raid. You know that the feds eventually released them. The now-sober Barkview residents figured they gave up Jonathan and ran them out of town."

I nodded. "That was the story I heard."

"They didn't. Jennifer found the old Prohibition interview files. Sally Tomlinson swore she lit two lanterns personally. Someone else sold out Jonathan. Whoever is trying to discredit Skye thinks she reported the wrong message."

"It doesn't answer who would blame Skye a hundred years later," I said.

"A Tomlinson, of course. After four generations, the names have changed, though."

Sandy had my attention.

"There were three Tomlinson brothers. One we know about went to San Pedro. Eventually he moved his family to Alaska. The second brother went to Canada. He continued to smuggle booze across the Great Lakes until 1930. Next generation went legitimate. They own a fish farm in Alberta. The last brother gave up the sea and moved to Colorado. They're a diverse lot, from forest rangers and environmentalists to lawyers and pot growers. One of the surnames in that branch is Thompson."

"Jordan Thompson?" My heart skipped a beat.

"One and the same. Jordan's PhD is from the University of Colorado–Boulder. Up until five years ago, he investigated egregious polluters for the EPA."

"And now he owns a dive shop in Barkview." No wonder Russ and I had sensed more. Was Barkview a magnet for witness protection? First Ariana and Chris and now possibly Jordan. Who else wasn't who they said they were?

"I'll find out what his last case was," Russ said, all business. "Great job, Sandy."

Sandy smiled. "Anytime. One more thing. Jennifer did some digging and it turns out the Land Trust is owned by the descendants of the Tomlinsons."

"Jordan," Russ and I said together. Time for another chat with the man in the morning. Sandy had earned the hop in her step tonight.

"Can you also check if Chad Williams has outstanding debts?" I asked.

"Other than student loans? They can be overwhelming."

True. Bark U wasn't cheap, but our scholarships were generous and Chad had been a teaching assistant until he graduated and became a junior professor last year. "I'm thinking it's more."

"Like gambling debts?" Sandy nodded. "Good luck with

your mom. I'd offer to go with you, but I value my life too much. Don't forget to rinse G-paw off before you pick her up. He's scratching his skin off."

Not to mention the none too pleasant wet dog aroma I'd noticed, even in the open-air boat.

I turned to Russ. "I'd better go." I had just enough time to get home, clean up, and pick up Mom. No time for G-paw's fooling around.

Russ took my face in both hands. My stomach twittered. "Do you want me to come with you to pick up your mother?"

He'd offered me a way out. Mom would never cause a scene with someone else nearby. Great as it sounded, I shook my head. "I need to do this alone."

"I understand. Know I'm here if you need me." His lips brushed mine with sweet promise. G-paw's head popped between us, breaking the mood. Sometimes, I swore that dog was on my mother's payroll.

CHAPTER 21

I fluffed G-paw's still-damp head as we paced at the bottom of the Terminal Two baggage claim escalator. The flight had landed on time. Mom preferred to sit in the back of the airplane, which always drove me crazy. I'd considered arriving later, but with my luck lately, she'd deviate from her routine.

That I deserved Mom's wrath didn't help any. I had failed to protect my little sister. I had no answers either. G-paw finally sat and just watched me pace until I saw an older, smaller version of myself approaching. Dressed in no-nonsense jeans and a blouse, her hair pulled back, she certainly looked like me.

My stomach flipped the moment we made eye contact. Was that relief I saw or just the transition into a deeper scowl?

No hug. No thank you. No greeting of any kind. Just a snarky "I see you're as informed as usual" that got right under my skin. Any wonder we barely spoke?

Although I felt it happening, I couldn't stop myself from responding. "As are you."

G-paw ended the standoff. He raised his right paw for a shake.

My mother's gasp was almost comical. "Good heavens. That's a dog."

I bit back my flippant reply. Mom shoved her hands in her pockets, refusing to even touch G-paw. I'd known she wasn't a particular fan of dogs, but this seemed extreme.

Not to be ignored, the Golden Doodle nudged her leg. She stepped back a foot. "That's G-paw," I said.

"Lani's G-paw?"

More like Peter's G-paw, but I wasn't ready for that explanation. "The same."

"But he's a d-dog."

At least we'd cleared that up. "You thought G-paw was a boyfriend?"

"They went everywhere together." Her confusion was real.

I tempered my chuckle. "Welcome to Barkview, Mom. It is the dog-friendliest place in America."

"After your experience, why would you ever have a...? Never mind. I don't want to know."

"But that's why you're here, isn't it? To lecture me on how completely I failed you?" G-paw's head bounced back and forth, watching us both, until he exhaled and leaned against me. My nerves instantly calmed, while Mom's red cheeks indicated her blood pressure was soaring. That wasn't healthy for either of us.

"Not here," she snapped and marched toward the baggage claim carousel.

I swear G-paw said "Huh" as we trailed behind her. Her good old passive aggressiveness never took long to get in the way. Finding Peter's killer was Lani's best chance at freedom. My sister needed me to focus. I didn't need to watch every word I said while Mother danced around our issues.

The similarity between Skye's relationship with her mother and my relationship with mine scared me. They'd been two strong, independent women, too alike for their own good, who'd royally failed to communicate. Years later, Skye regretted her rift with her mother. I didn't want that. Somehow, I needed to control my defensiveness. Mom wasn't always attacking me. She just made it sound that way. Where to start...

Watching checked luggage go round and round the carousel turned out to be therapeutic. Each bag had a tag reading SAN. Some had additional three-letter transfer point tags. DFW for Dallas–Fort Worth came up as often as HNL for Honolulu. Wait a minute. Airline city and country codes were all three letters. Madame Orr's prophecy claimed the truth was hidden behind a lie, or did she mean L-I-E?

I quick googled the LIE code. Liechtenstein. Another piece fell into place. Skye's aircraft design collaboration with a British aeronautics company began at Vaduz Castle in Liechtenstein in the early 1930s.

"I know how to help Lani." Anticipation hummed through me. I knew the location of the missing diary.

If Mom recognized my ready-to-explode excitement, she said nothing. She just pointed out her three extra-large suitcases.

"How long are you planning on staying?" I nearly pulled a groin muscle from the sheer weight of the bag. Thank goodness it was on wheels.

"As long as it takes." She meant it too.

Ugh! I refused to succumb to panic. I had a plan. I focused on that.

"How can we help Lani?" she asked as we loaded the luggage into my SUV and climbed in. G-paw wisely jumped in the back and lay across the seat, alert but quiet.

Her use of "we" could mean anything. "It's a long story." I didn't even know where to start.

"Start your story," Mom said, stopping my next excuse, "at the beginning."

An explanation would keep our conversation neutral for the forty-minute ride up the coast to Barkview. What wasn't to like about that?

I backed my car out of the parking stall and headed home. She'd asked for it. "It started in 1922 with an independent young woman who was destined to fly airplanes." I told Mom a mini-version of Skye's story, from the disappearance of Jonathan Douglas and his namesake diamond to Skye's remarkable accomplishments and how someone was trying to undermine her induction into the National Aviation Hall of Fame. (I skipped the part about the Romas. That wasn't my story to tell yet.)

"A Tomlinson is behind it," Mom stated matter-of-factly.

She'd nailed that one fast. Had I inherited my intuition from Mom? "Unfortunately, we have no evidence."

"The attacks are personal. This is about payback. Mark my words."

"The Tomlinsons moved away a hundred years ago. They made lives elsewhere. It makes no sense."

"They were driven away. Revenge isn't logical or necessarily timely."

She had a point. "Hopefully, I'll know as soon as I have Skye's missing diary."

"Why do you think it's hidden behind an L.I.E. sticker?" Mom asked.

"Madame Orr said..." I didn't bite my tongue in time.

"Lani's psychic?" Her who-are-you-and-what-have-you-done-with-my-daughter expression had "impossible" written all over it.

My cheeks must've been cherry-red. "It's complicated. Lani is the, uh, regular."

"The Moon card is..."

Not the same old argument. "Let's agree to disagree on this, okay?"

She nodded, oddly not miffed. Maybe she wanted peace as badly as I did.

"How does Lani fit into all of this?" Mom asked.

I yoga-breathed. Now for the hard part. Peter and G-paw's tale took less time, but elicited more recriminations from her. I finished with, "Someone has gone to great lengths to frame Lani."

"Thank you for that." Mom took a deep breath. "Is this about Michael?"

Knock me over. Mom even considering her perfect husband could be to blame? I still rushed to reassure her. "Russ doesn't think so."

I felt her beseeching look. "And you trust him?"

"With my life."

Mom patted my hand. "That's all that matters. He's a good man, Cat."

"He is. You'll meet him."

"I have. He flew to Hawaii and asked Michael and me for our blessing to marry you. I'm surprised he never told you."

I should be mad. Oddly, I wasn't. My crazy familial relationship wouldn't alter his code. Russ always did the right thing, and in doing so had made this moment possible with my mother. I smiled.

I drove directly to Aunt Char's house. She and Renny met us on the front steps of the antebellum mansion the moment I pulled up. "You just get younger, Mary Ann." Aunt Char wrapped my mom in a perfumed hug.

"And you just get more beautiful, Charlotte."

I didn't exactly understand their strange ritual, and neither woman would explain it. "You two can catch up. I have a diary to find." G-paw nudged me aside as he bounded for the front door, until Renny's sharp bark stopped him like a brick wall. G-paw shook his head and sat beside me, his wary eye on the haughty Cavalier.

A snack in the world of Golden Doodles, the queen Cavalier had proven yet again that attitude matters. A lesson I needed to master with this exuberant and act-before-you-think dog. Renny gave me the get-your-act-together head toss and regally led us inside. G-paw minded perfectly as we climbed the grand staircase. I took the lead at the top stair, leaving Renny behind as G-paw and I raced up the attic stairs. He won by a lot. I found him stretched out in front of Skye's metal Belber wardrobe trunk.

I circled the case's perimeter. I was on the right track. I knew it. Skye's pendant just about felt like a glowing coal on my chest. Sure enough, tucked beside the Hotel Somerset London label was the LIE tag on the trunk's outer edge. I ran my finger across the label, feeling the solid metal underneath. I thumb-pressed the whole area but found no concealed switch to open a hidden compartment.

I felt rather than saw Aunt Char and my mother behind me. "I was so sure." Disappointment threatened.

Aunt Char circled the trunk. "Your great-grandmother Emma Wright had a trunk similar to this. It had an interior false back."

Hope stirred as I opened the trunk. I ignored the side with multiple compartments and focused instead on the hanging garments. A brown leather bomber jacket with tarnished brass buttons and a khaki safari coat with matching long shorts came out first.

"I can hold them." My mother offered her arms, and I laid

the garments across them.

Next, I removed a form-fitting red qipao with an elaborate trail of embroidered birds down one side. I piled on full-length beaded evening dresses, shorter flapper styles, wide-legged pants, and flowing silk blouses that spoke of high-society parties until I could barely see her eyes.

Sure enough, behind the clothing I located another LIE tag. I ran my fingers over this seal and felt a familiar indentation immediately.

Skye's charm really was a key. I removed the pendant from around my neck and pressed it into the indentation. I turned it to the left.

Both Aunt Char and my mom breathed down my neck as they looked over my shoulder. Inside the small compartment I found a brown leather book, cracked with age and use, and a replica of the charm I'd used to open the compartment rubber-banded on top.

"You found it." Was that awe in my mother's voice?

"Of course she did. Never a doubt." Aunt Char's businesslike tone confirmed her statement.

G-paw barked his agreement.

I stilled my shaking hands as I opened the book. Skye's familiar script sent a warm-chocolate-chip-cookie kind of feeling through me. Aloud I read:

Property of Skye Barklay. May the information contained be used for the good of those involved. I write these pages forty-seven days after the June 25, 1925, Santa Barbara earthquake with a heavy heart. Barkview will never be the same. So many lies, so much pain. Here is the truth.

Good or bad, I'd finally know. My heart pounded as I turned to the next page.

CHAPTER 22

"Stop, Cat. As mayor, I prefer to hear revelations seated," Aunt Char announced.

I opened my mouth to argue. Seriously, was I the only one eaten alive with impatience?

"Let us reconvene in the family parlor." Aunt Char left no options in that suggestion.

My mother added, "And don't peek, Cat. We would all like to hear this together."

On notice by both of them? Had to be a conspiracy. Who didn't read the last page of a mystery first?

I pouted while I helped Mom rehang Skye's garments, then followed her downstairs where Renny lay stretched out at the bottom step, ready for the big reveal. I swear that dog knew sitting out the dust bunnies wouldn't cause her to miss a thing. G-paw at least felt my pain and nudged me to rush the process.

I'd always called this family gathering place with its sweeping view of the backyard gardens the Cavalier Room, mostly because every pillow and portrait depicted Barklay Cavalier champions.

Aunt Char went right to the bar. "Shall we be civilized?" She mixed a martini, poured a glass, and hand it to my mother. "Extra dry, Mary Ann. Just the way you like it."

"You know me too well."

My mother held her glass and waited as Aunt Char popped a cork and poured champagne for us both. G-paw eyed Renny and snorted when he thought she wasn't looking. The Cavalier's huff put him right back in his place.

Aunt Char held up her glass. "To remarkable ladies."

Now that was worth drinking to. I guzzled the celebratory champagne, refusing to waste a minute more on civility when answers burned at my fingertips.

Aloud I read:

June 25, 1925

Mother locked me in my room. I couldn't get out until too late. Jonathan was counting on me to fly reconnaissance tonight. Crack will cover for me. He always does when Mother gets difficult. The caves are empty except for some special bottles of Mother's brandy. Jonathan showed me a sketch of the diamond necklace he purchased for Marie.

The British ship has brought it from London. I can't wait to see it. Marie will be pleased. Crack said he had a surprise for me too. I hope it's new fuses.

Crack's been shot. Although a single light was on at Sally Tomlinson's, G-men were waiting on the beach. Why? Sally could see the police. Crack ordered me to go to my brother's house. It's the only place I'll be safe. The police will make an example out of a Barklay.

Crack gave me an envelope and said, "Mi Cielo Azul. My

son will find you," and shoved me out the bolt-hole as the
Red Door crashed in.

I stood with my brother and his family in the yard as the
earthquake rolled through Barkview. Buildings collapsed
and glass shattered around me like my life. My brother
stopped me from going back for Crack.

July 5, 1925
The law never came for me. Crack protected me. They
arrested and deported him. The government called him a
subversive anarchist. His injury was bad. He would say he
has survived worse. At least he is home with his wife and son
now. She will care for him. Someday we will fly together
again. I miss my friend.

Jonathan evaded capture. Only a pile of rocks remain of the
smuggling caves. The floatplane is gone too, buried inside. If
Jonathan was inside, he did not survive. Hope he hid in
another cave fades daily. Only Marie believes he still lives.
Most blamed Sally Tomlinson for Jonathan's death, but I'm
not sure. She had no motive. Jonathan supplied her brandy
and Sally loved her brandy.

July 10, 1925
Mother demands I marry Bradley Oldeman. He hates dogs.
Can you imagine? I don't love him. I don't even like him. I
will never marry him. Mother can disinherit me. I'm a
pilot. I will fly.

July 11, 1925
I visited Edna at her family's home. She is marrying a hotel
man from Chicago. I don't understand why. She doesn't love

him. Does she just want to leave Barkview? It is a sad place with Jonathan still missing and the wild Tomlinsons gone. Is Jonathan in hiding or lost forever? What happened to Marie's necklace?

The G-men released the Tomlinsons, but they have been convicted in the court of public opinion. Mother says they gave the government evidence for their freedom. It makes no sense. It doesn't feel right that they betrayed Jonathan.

Edna's smugness doesn't seem right either. She'd been at Sally's house on the night of the earthquake. She could've lit the all-clear light. Why would she do it? She loved Jonathan.

July 12, 1925
Marie's heart is broken. She is so pale and thin. She told me she is with child. The son Jonathan always prayed for. She'd planned to tell him on their anniversary. She must eat for the baby.

July 13, 1925
Edna betrayed Jonathan and the Tomlinsons. She admitted it herself. She did it in jealousy because of Jonathan's child. If she couldn't have him, no one would. I am torn between loyalty to a friend and what is right. Mother says I can't betray my future family. Is that why Bradley has agreed to marry me? To protect Edna? The Oldeman family doesn't deserve to pay for Edna's deeds. She should pay for her own mistakes.

I can't keep quiet about this. The Tomlinsons have been

banished for no reason. Edna doesn't deserve a new life in Chicago when she has ruined so many.

July 15, 1925
I told Sheriff Smythe of Edna's crimes. He doesn't care. He lectured me on family loyalty. Edna is marrying an important man and leaving town. Edna will never see justice.

Edna's groom has left Barkview. I had to tell him. Mother is angry. Bradley is angry. I don't care. Tory Rose understands. She always understands.

July 31, 1925
I finally found the courage to open the envelope Crack gave me on the night of the earthquake. Inside was the sketch of the plane we'd designed. The note said: "La Ciela Azula is your destiny. Be true to yourself and follow your dreams." The plane is at the Ryan Airfield waiting for me with a suitcase full of rumrunning money—my share Crack had kept for my future. I fell in love the moment I saw her sleek silver body and edged wings. The money made my decision easier. I took off without a backward glance. I'll miss Tory Rose. She'll understand.

"Wow!" What else could I say? Hollywood couldn't have written a better script.

"Congratulations, my dear. You rewrote Barkview history tonight," Aunt Char said.

"In the end the Tomlinsons were unfairly banished. I suppose I understand an ancestor's anger, but Skye shouldn't be punished for doing the right thing either." My sense of right hit all cylinders now.

"How does this help Lani?" My mother asked the key question.

"Peter was Crack's great-great-grandson. The Tomlinson descendant attacking Skye has been after this diary. Russ and I need to talk to Jordan."

Aunt Char nodded, unruffled as usual. "So, Jordan Thompson is a Tomlinson. As Barklay will become Hawl when you inherit, the names have all changed, but Barkview's foundation remains true. You will stay with me, Mary Ann. We have an engagement party to plan."

I expected an argument from my mother, not acquiescence or pride in her smile. "Be careful, Catalina. We are not going to end up like Skye and her mother," she whispered as she hugged me at the door.

As I drove past 335 Rock Road, I realized I believed her. Russ and I would build a life together in that house, with my mother and sister playing their part. Skye had seen to it.

CHAPTER 23

I parked beside Russ at the Bark U Science building in front of the stone steps. At night the bustling quad filled with youthful idealism transformed into a forbidding Ivy League structure. G-paw felt it too. He stutter-stepped on the passenger seat, literally biting at his leash to get out. I'd walked him before driving over, so this anxiety had to be about the coming meeting.

Good thing Russ opened my door for me. He caught G-paw mid-dash out the door. "Whoa, man. Not yet." Russ soothed the dog with calm hands I'd rather have liked on myself. "How'd it go with your mother?"

Too long a story for now. So I used his words. "Imagine my surprise when I discovered my fiancé secretly has met with my mother."

No apology from Russ. Not that I expected one. He never apologized for doing the right thing. I did note tension framing his mouth, though. "Thank you," I said.

"You're welcome. Time to focus." He visibly relaxed.

"I'm glad you put eyes on Jordan." I might chafe at losing

control of the investigation, but only a little. The diligence of many far exceeded the abilities of the ego of one.

"I'd never have guessed Jordan's first call after meeting with us would be the Bark U Science department."

"We have the link between Chad and Jordan now." We'd both believed Jordan's plea. Talk about a confidence shaker.

"Jordan's reason for leaving the EPA is listed as family-related," Russ explained. "It appears you were right about Chad's financial problems as well."

"Excesses?"

"Not as nefarious or selfish as you'd hoped. His mother is undergoing experimental cancer treatments in Mexico."

"Not covered by insurance, I guess." I really wanted to hate him. I just couldn't in this case. I understood desperation and family.

Russ couldn't either. His reluctant nod to campus security to grant us entry into the building said it all. I noted a pair from Russ's surveillance team covering our flank as we entered. G-paw heeled to Russ's command as our footsteps echoed down the tiled hallway. I smelled clean pine as we took the stairs to the second floor. A light outlining Chad's office door drew us closer, but Jordan's booming voice stopped us.

"What have you done?" Anger vibrated through Jordan's tone.

"Relax. They have nothing." A woman's voice? That wasn't Chad Williams. Who else would have access to his office?

"It's not nothing when Cat Wright and Russ Hawl catch you diving on the X on a dead man's treasure map," Jordan insisted.

It felt good to be in the same category as super-investigator Russ. Jordan continued, "It's been a hundred years since the Tomlinsons' exodus. Reestablishing our history is the goal. We all agreed. You have no right to jeopardize the plan to pursue your own agenda."

A murmur agitated Jordan further. "And incriminating that girl and me by taking my foxglove. I knew it was you. You left your gloves. I want no part of this vendetta." He gasped. "Marilyn, put that away. I'm your cousin. You're not going to shoot me."

He had to be talking to Dr. Thomas, the dean of the Science Department. We'd heard more than enough for a search warrant. I looked to Russ for our next move. He itched to break down the door. Since I'd been in there before, I warned him, "The room is a converted closet. There are only a few feet between the door and the desk."

G-paw decided our next move. Although he'd behaved up until that point, the dog suddenly jerked the leash out of Russ's hand and nosed open the only partly-closed door. Growling like an out-for-blood guard dog, he lunged inside.

Ready or not. Russ motioned our backup to move in, pulled out his weapon, and followed. Heart pounding, I didn't think, just set my phone to record video and joined them. I plowed right into Russ's back, dropping my phone when the first shot whizzed by my ear. OMG! Not target practice again!

Instinctively, I dropped to the ground, smacking my already-tender knee on the tile. Russ piled on top, shielding and squashing me. I'd feel that in the morning. Jordan lay on the floor beside me, blood soaking through his T-shirt. A lot of it.

We were pinned in the four feet separating the door from the desk, with no place to go and a gunwoman standing on the other side of the desk above us. G-paw fearlessly held his ground, Doberman-growling at her feet. The woman's string of expletives would offend a seasoned sailor. "Come out or I shoot the dog," she finally screamed.

My heart jumped into my throat. Not that lovable, rambunctious dog who deserved a loving home. I poked Russ's shoulder and pointed under the desk. He had a direct shot at the woman's foot. Not a life-threatening injury, but a major distraction.

Russ nodded. He had a plan. I could tell. He signaled me to distract her as he crept around the corner and into harm's way. I sucked in my breath, terrified he'd be shot.

"Dr. Thomas, I presume." I saw her reflection in a wall mirror.

Dressed all in black and wearing gold-rimmed glasses, the dean of the Bark U Science Department seemed too ordinary to be a danger. Of course, the 9 mm said otherwise, as did as the wildness in her blue eyes—a crazy obsessiveness, really.

"Of the Colorado Tomlinsons. Are you Jordan's cousin?" I needed to keep her talking. She had a gun aimed at G-paw.

I could do this. I filled air space all the time when filming at KDOG. "I have Skye's diary describing the government raid. You are welcome to read it."

My words sank in. She responded, "You will lie to protect a Barklay. The rich never pay for their crimes."

Her emphatic *never* indicated a deeper significance. My short laugh got her attention. "You don't know me very well, Dr. Thomas. I report the truth—everyone knows that. Don't I, Jordan?

"She does, Marilyn. Everyone knows Cat Wright reports with integrity." His weak words didn't bode well for recovery if Russ and I didn't hurry this standoff along.

"For the record, Skye did not betray your family. She fought for justice."

"I don't believe you. Skye didn't fly the recon flight that night."

"You're right, Crack did. Is that why you killed Peter? Because of his great-great-grandfather?"

"Peter Gallardo killed my twin sister."

Talk about a bomb. That announcement came out of nowhere. I had no idea what to say.

Russ filled in. "You are Elena Thomas's sister. My condolences. She was in the wrong place."

"She shouldn't have been at the dam that night. She was doing a favor for a friend." Dr. Thomas's wistful tone could signal progress.

"It was a tragedy," Russ agreed. "Peter was never prosecuted."

"Because of his rich grandfather." Marilyn's voice cracked. "He paid this time."

OMG! Had she just admitted to murdering Peter? It didn't make sense. I glanced at Jordan. He wasn't looking good.

"You are wrong about Peter," Russ said.

"I was not. He was there. I know he was there."

"He was there. Peter was the FBI informant who ultimately brought down the perpetrators," Russ informed us.

Peter, a hero? Lani had been right about him all along. More troubling was Russ telling agency secrets. He never did that. Were we in worse shape than I'd thought?

"Good job, cuz. You killed one of the good ones!" Jordan grimaced, his complexion now ashen.

"No. He was guilty." Did Marilyn Thomas's voice sound less sure?

"Peter spent three months recovering from injuries after reporting the bombing," Russ explained. "He nearly died protecting the ecosystem."

"Which explains why he was available to teach at Bark U on short notice," Jordan added. He was breathing hard now.

Too many puzzle pieces remained missing. "How did you

know about Peter's interest in Barkview?" It couldn't have just been a coincidence he'd ended up here. Could it?

"He applied for positions all over San Diego. When I looked into his past, I knew he had a link to Barkview." That righteous gleam in her eyes seemed unreal.

"How did you know about the Digoxin?" I asked.

"Peter disclosed his heart condition in our interview." Marilyn had developed a complex plan for her revenge.

"You could've killed him at any time. Why now?" I asked. But I knew the answer. The 1939 C-Cap Land Cover Atlas I'd glimpsed on Chad's desk when we barged in told that story. "You waited to see if Peter could find the Douglas Diamond. You instigated the competition between Peter and Chad. Didn't you?"

"What better way to return to Barkview than with the Douglas Diamond?" Marilyn replied.

"Along the way, you found the perfect scapegoat in my sister. You thought you'd get away with it."

Her narrowed eyes proved my hypothesis.

"Your mistake was trying to set up my sister."

"With her powerful friends, she never should've spent a day in custody. You failed her."

I'd actually just freed her. I suddenly got Marilyn's point. "You searched her dorm to throw suspicion elsewhere, didn't you? Why mess with the perfect setup?"

"Your sister is guilty of naivete. She doesn't deserve to pay for a crime she didn't commit," Marilyn admitted. "I'd be a hypocrite to think otherwise."

Honor in insanity? "Why did you come to Barkview?"

Jordan answered, albeit weakly. "Our grandmother always claimed our family was wrongly run out of Barkview. When the ninety-nine-year Barkview land lease ended on the north shore property and it reverted to our family, we decided to reclaim our heritage. This"—he gestured to Marilyn—"will prove Barkview is better off without us."

Maybe a tad melodramatic. "Marilyn's crimes are her own. Skye's diary exonerates Sally. Edna Oldeman, Sally Tomlinson's companion, admitted to extinguishing the smuggler's abort signal. It was never about the Tomlinsons. Edna was in love with Jonathan and couldn't accept his loss." Talk about an insane jealous rage.

"An Oldeman did it." Marilyn seemed to slump.

I kept talking. "And paid for it. They lost the Old Barkview Inn after the 1929 crash. You can thank Skye for that. She inadvertently caused that when she refused to marry Bradley Oldeman and left town."

"The Barklay money would've saved them," Marilyn said.

"Perhaps. Your family was wrongly accused. Barkview will correct that. While we can't give you back one hundred years, we can welcome the Tomlinsons home. We start by recognizing the cannery as a historic site."

"Why?" Was that a tear in her wild eyes?

"Skye wanted the truth told. I promise you it will be."

"I believe you will, Cat Wright." With that, Marilyn Thomas relinquished her weapon without firing another shot.

I ran into Russ's arms as his team zip-tied her arms behind her back. G-paw leaned against us both, sharing the love.

Marilyn had wanted justice. I understood that. So did Russ. Made me wonder just how far we would go to do the same. What had happened to the Tomlinsons would never happen on our watch.

After all the revelations, the fact that the Douglas Diamond remained lost bothered me most. At least I knew the stone was not just lore perpetuated by a grief-stricken woman and a wannabe king's prophecy. Problem was, where should we look for it? We'd investigated every tangible lead, current and past.

Did that secret romantic beach even exist? Could I reign in my impatience until the Santa Ana wind created the right conditions to lead us to the treasure?

Did I have a choice? In the meantime, KDOG needed to be run, and I had a wedding to plan. Oh, and a movie was coming to town. That ought to keep me busy.

Lani would be released soon. What to do with G-paw suddenly became an issue.

CHAPTER 24

"Peter dognapped G-paw?" Was Peter Gallardo a hero or a bum? Or, like most of us, just a complex individual?

That Lani hadn't been surprised did bother me, though. How many more secrets hadn't she shared?

"Not exactly. Peter found G-paw a few days before moving to Barkview. He just didn't return the dog when he found out who was looking for him. In all fairness, Peter had already moved," Sandy explained.

"That's no excuse. G-paw wasn't his to keep." I'd figured that out a few days ago; maybe I'd sensed that longing to find his family and go home.

"G-paw's owner is at the Old Barkview Inn right now. Apparently, he flew out of Dallas on the first flight he could get a seat on."

"He's not taking any chances." What else could I say? I scratched the dog's head. It really was over.

"You're going to like Mitch Felderhoff. His family manufactures healthy dog food," Sandy insisted.

"That explains why G-paw's a grazer."

Sandy nodded. "He is the official company taster. In fact, Mitch is a character too. To prove his dog food is healthy, he ate it for thirty days."

"What?" Ick.

"You heard me."

I wish I hadn't.

"Seriously, the food is super-healthy. I'll send you his Facebook link and this cool YouTube interview. It's a riot. He and G-paw are a pair."

Of what, I couldn't answer. They clearly belonged together. More proof owners and dogs were linked. Why did it still hurt so much?

"By the way, G-paw's name is really Grandpa Joe. Mitch named him after his grandfather. There's a story there, too, I'm sure. You should ask him about it."

Not likely. I would be bawling my eyes out.

In the end, Russ drove me to the inn to return G-paw. I guess I didn't trust myself to actually do it either. About a block from the hotel, the Golden Doodle started barking. Not a high-pitched annoying bark, but the I've-got-a-new-stick bark.

When Russ opened the car door, the dog leaped right over me from the back seat and bolted into the Old Barkview Inn. We abandoned the car at the valet and sprinted after him. Visions of overturned antique vases about stopped my heart. That dog seemed intent on bankrupting me.

No need to worry. We found Grandpa Joe in the lobby bar licking a blue-eyed man into a slobbery mess. I about cracked then and there. Russ pulled me into his embrace. "Grandpa Joe's been looking for Mitch everywhere. He's home now."

He certainly was. I pinky-wiped the tears from my eyes. I would miss Grandpa Joe's goofy head shakes and silly antics. He made me laugh in crises and comforted me when I needed it. The mind-of-his-own behavior was troublesome, though, and sharing my food didn't work too well for me.

I thought about the dog charm bracelet with four charms. Something told me this journey wasn't over yet. No sense looking for trouble. We still had the Douglas Diamond to find.

"So, what's your next move?" Russ asked.

I looked up into my fiancé's heart-thumping baby-blue eyes. "Think I'll just enjoy the view."

Russ cupped my face in his hands. "Me too," he whispered, and kissed me.

The End 🐾🐾🐾🐾

I hope you enjoyed your adventure in the dog-friendliest place in America. To learn more about Barkview and Cat's next adventure, visit www.cbwilsonauthor.com.

Sign up for **The Bark View**, a monthly update on all things Barkview, including

- *Friday Funnies*: pet-related cartoons
- Recipes from *Bichon Bisquets Barkery's* canine kitchen
- Cool merchandise ideas from the *Bow Wow Boutique*
- Not to mention Barkview news and fun contests.

Join Cat on her quest for the perfect dog when she teams up with a Corgi to solve a World War II mystery and find the long-lost Douglas Diamond in **Corgied to Death**.

COMING SOON: CORGIED TO DEATH

The hunt for the elusive Douglas Diamond continues with the murder of a respected Centurion, who leaves a tell-all diary accusing a prominent political family of a World War II cover-up that strikes at the foundation of Barkview's elite. Has the tale of the Douglas Diamond just been an elaborate hoax to hide an eighty-year-old conspiracy?

When the FBI arrests a shady movie location scout, it's game over. Except events begin mirroring the Douglas Diamond's prophecy, and Cat Wright realizes the real answers lie in the past.

With her Corgi helper at her side, Cat must right a long-ignored wrong before the window to find the diamond closes forever.

ACKNOWLEDGMENTS

To my writing cheerleaders Pam Wright, Dee Kaler, Bill Hubiak, Becky Witters, and Brandi Wilson, who endlessly listen to my ideas, edit my spelling and grammar, help research and test recipes, thank you.

For research and police procedure assistance, thank you to Richard R. Zitzke, Chief of Police, Whitehall, Ohio, retired. I assure you any errors are entirely my fault.

Thank you to Melissa Martin. You keep me sane.

To Kim Homa, Eddie Hale, Mitch Felderhoff and Grandpa Joe. You all inspired me. Anyone willing to eat their own dog food for a month is a character in my book.

About the Author

C.B. Wilson's love of writing began after she read her first Nancy Drew book and reworked the ending. Studying at the Gemology Institute of America, she discovered a passion for researching lost, stolen, and missing diamonds. The big kind. Her fascination with dogs and their passionate owners inspired Barkview, California, the dog-friendliest city in America.

C.B. lives in Peoria, Arizona, with her husband. She is an avid pickleball player who enjoys traveling to play tournaments. She admits to chocoholic tendencies and laughing out loud at dog comics.

Connect with C.B. Wilson at www.cbwilsonauthor.com
Facebook: www.facebook.com/cbwilsonauthor
Instagram: www.instagram.com/cbwilsonauthor

AUTHOR'S NOTE

Early female aviators, called "aviatrixes," intrigued me. As I began research for *Doodled to Death*, I knew I needed to write about a brave Barklay woman who beat the aviation odds. The first female to earn a pilot's license was Harriet Quimby in 1911. In 1928 only twelve women held licenses. The 1929 National Women's Air Derby was the first of its kind. Fourteen of twenty pilots completed the twenty-eight-hundred-mile race. In the 1930s there were women wing-walkers, daredevils, and stunt flyers. By World War II, one thousand women flew over sixty million miles ferrying aircraft and personnel. They did not fly in combat missions until 1993.

The Curtiss Model R Floatplane did have a fold-up wing model, and yes, World War I "crack" pilots did fly for Mexican independence. Using airplanes for bootlegging was a thing during Prohibition.

While the California coastline does have ocean caves, the Barkview subterranean tunnels are not real.

Although FDR's New Deal did include major dam projects

in southern California, the project that changed the Barkview Lagoon is my invention.

Mitch Felderhoff really did eat Muenster dog food for thirty days and the health benefits were life changing. Check the results out at https://www.youtube.com/watch?v=3Q_FPP slCWs.

Made in the USA
Las Vegas, NV
12 April 2023

70483484R00121